NOTORIOUS

K.M. SCOTT

BOOKS BY K.M. SCOTT

Crash Into Me (Heart of Stone #1)

Fall Into Me (Heart of Stone #2)

Give In To Me (Heart of Stone #3)

Heart of Stone Volume One

Ever After (Heart of Stone #4)

A Heart of Stone Christmas (Heart of Stone #5)

Return To Me (Heart of Stone #6)

Forever With Me (Heart of Stone #7)

Heart of Stone Volume Two

Hard As Stone (Heart of Stone #8)

Set In Stone (Heart of Stone #9)

Silent As A Stone (Heart of Stone #10)

Heart of Stone Volume Three

All of Me (Heart of Stone #11)

Temptation (Club X #1)

Surrender (Club X #2)

Possession (Club X #3)

Satisfaction (Club X #4)

Acceptance (Club X #5)

Complete Club X Series

Notorious

Cade March loves his life. Free to do as he likes and wealthy enough to afford whatever his heart desires, he's all about having fun.

As the only son of Stefan March, he's the spitting image of his father in every way.

And that's the problem. At least for everyone else.

Hailey Canton lives a very different life. Still recovering from a betrayal that's left her shaken and no longer believing in love, she only has the desserts she makes for her parents' small restaurant to make her feel like she can do anything.

The cakes and cookies she lovingly creates are works of art, but to her, they're simply a lifeline so she doesn't give up.

What happens when the very thing she's feared comes into her life in the form of a gorgeous man with no idea that life has any limits and who fears nothing?

Publisher's Note: Notorious is the first book in Cade and Hailey's duet. This book ends on a cliffhanger. Their story concludes in Infamous.

2021 Copper Key Media LLC

Published in the United States

ISBN: 978-1-7346645-9-1

CHAPTER ONE

ade

"THIS IS THE LIFE. YOU KNOW THAT?" I SAY AS I weave in between cars on my way to nowhere in particular.

It's a gorgeous spring day that would be a crime to waste inside, so Alex and I are riding around listening to music and enjoying the freedom that comes from being single guys beholden to not a damn soul.

When I glance to my right, I see him nod his head and lean back in the passenger seat of my Jag. Closing his eyes, he says, "It's days like this that make going to work hard as fuck sometimes. Thank God I don't have to go in today. The last thing I want to do is spend an eight hour stretch slaving in that kitchen."

"I don't know how you do it. Really, I don't. If I had to work with my father and uncle day in and day out, I'd kill someone. I'd turn into one of those guys who goes on a rampage and then when the cops and the news talk to the neighbors, they always say things like, 'He was a quiet guy. Never bothered anyone. I can't believe he took a meat cleaver and hacked up an entire kitchen staff and both the owners of such a fine restaurant. I just can't.'"

Alex laughs at my imitation of every next-door neighbor ever seen on the news talking about some homicidal maniac who lived next to them. "Yeah, and they always have that look on their faces like they really can't believe that was the guy who lived in the blue house across the street. 'He looked so nice. I swear I never knew.'"

I take the corner hard onto a side street and chuckle. "They just can't believe their dumb luck that the crazy guy who snapped didn't come over and kill them that time they let him borrow the weed whacker."

"My favorite is when they say things like, 'It's such a shame. He comes from such a good family. I know his mother. She's a very nice lady.' As if that's why he's a mass murderer. Like it's in the genes."

That thought rolls around my head for a minute. Is there some DNA marker for mass murderer? I don't think so. Not that I've ever heard of, but maybe. Anything's possible.

If that's the base, though, the whole lot of us in my family would be screwed. My mind wanders to the idea of seven mass murderers. That would be something. A whole family of killers.

Although I can't imagine Ava even killing a fly, and Annalea doesn't seem to have the killer instinct in her either. Wilder's definitely got it. That's for sure. But he's not blood, even if he is part of the family.

"Hey! Pull over into that restaurant," Alex says, ripping me from my thoughts about the March and Jackson family's potential as killers.

"What?"

I look around and don't see anywhere we'd want to go. Just some diner that makes me think I can taste the grease by just looking at the place. He can't want to go there. Alex is a chef, for God's sake. There's no way he wants to eat at this greasy spoon.

Pointing at the very building I'm sure he can't want to go to, he repeats himself. "Pull over! Let's stop in that restaurant."

He looks like he's going to practically jump out of the car while it's still moving he's so eager to get to this diner. What the hell did I miss?

"Relax. It's not like the place is going to disappear before I get the car parked. Jesus. You'd swear this is some five star restaurant. It's a diner. I would have thought you hated these kinds of places."

I look up at the sign as I pull into the parking lot. Comfort Food. Catchy name for a dive. They probably have things like meatloaf and grilled cheese sandwiches on the menu. Not exactly what I ever pegged Alex being into.

When I stop the car and kill the engine, I look over to see him flinging the door open. "Wait! Why are we here? You have a craving for some fried food or something?"

He shrugs like I'm making a big deal out of nothing. "Not really, but don't worry. It'll be fine. This place has great desserts."

Before I can ask when he became such a big dessert fan, he jumps out of the car and slams the door. Great desserts, huh? By the looks of the building, I'd be surprised. Gunmetal grey block walls with silver trim around the windows makes me wonder if he's gotten this place mistaken with somewhere else.

I walk toward the entrance and mumble, "You'd think at somewhere called Comfort Food the outside wouldn't look like I was walking into some dive bar off a dusty highway. Doesn't feel very comforting to me."

By the time I find him, he's all settled into a booth complete with silver seats that have a distinct pleather vibe to them. It's not pleather, though. By the way the seat squeaks as I slide into the booth, I know it's vinyl.

"Is this place going for some retro vibe or something? I feel like there should be a jukebox somewhere around here. You know the kind with actual little records in them. Forty-fives I think is what they were called."

Alex taps his knuckles on the table. "Check it out. Real, honest to goodness Formica! Definitely retro. I love it."

I arch one eyebrow and study him suspiciously, sure someone has stolen my best friend and replaced him with this hipster sitting across from me admiring the white Formica table with silver and gold designs that look like the nuclear symbol. He actually traces the design with his fingertip, like he's enchanted by it.

"Remember in fifth grade when the teacher told us all about fallout shelters. That's what that looks like. Not a good omen for a food place. Radiation poisoning on the menu?" I joke.

He looks up at me and scowls. "It's not a nuclear symbol. I think it's got more of a Star Trek vibe with the two swooshes, one silver and one gold."

Sitting back against the silver vinyl behind me, I shake my head. "You're sort of freaking me out here, Alex. I was worried that maybe being a serial killer runs in our family, but now I'm more worried about whatever you're exhibiting at this moment."

Alex rolls his eyes and goes back to studying the oh-so-interesting ancient table. "Do you remember that server I was seeing a while back? She was into all that fifties stuff big time, so I got to know a little about it. That's all."

My mind wanders back to which girlfriend of his he could be talking about, but there have been a lot, so I can't be blamed for not recalling this particular one. "Which one? The girl who had the Minnie Mouse obsession and loved to wear those big bows in her hair? That, by the way, was bizarre. If you hadn't told me she was a freak in bed, I would have thought you lost your mind going out with her in public."

His dark eyebrows come in toward his nose as he makes that pissed off look he gives me any time he's really angry at something I've said. "No, I don't mean Misty, asshole. And she wasn't that bad with those bows. She just liked dressing up sometimes. You didn't like her because of her friend."

Ugh. That I do remember.

Shaking my head, I try to get rid of the image of her best friend Sandi and her ruby red lips plastered with lipstick. "Damn. How did I let you talk me into going out with her that time? You still owe me for that, and since you made me remember her, you owe me twice. Dude, that was a nightmare."

"Well, you brought up Misty. That's on you, not me. But I wasn't talking about her. I was talking about Tori. You remember. She had black hair and she wore it in that way that pin-up models from the fifties did."

I vaguely have a sense of who he's talking about, but because I can't get Sandi and that horrible lipstick that tasted like plastic when I kissed her out of my mind, I don't think I can focus on anything now. Alex's taste in women runs the gamut from wild to utterly bizarre. It's so odd too because he doesn't look like he'd go for anyone other than hot women, but he's got a thing for the strange ones.

"She's not really registering with me at the moment, but it's fine. I'm glad she expanded your horizons regarding the fifties diner style."

"Just open your mind, okay? The pastry chef here makes the most phenomenal desserts. My father and Kane tried to woo her to come work at CK a few months ago, but she wouldn't even take their calls."

Looking around at the diner and wondering why we don't even have menus yet since there are no more than two other booths filled with customers, I doubt this place even has a pastry chef. That's probably just Alex throwing around his chef lingo again. Nobody's just a cook with him. Everybody's some kind of chef. Pastry chef. Sous chef. Executive chef. The person making desserts here is probably just some schlub who knows how to slap on some frosting on a cake.

A server finally makes her way over to our table a minute later. All smiles and very pretty, she looks about seventeen, if that. When she opens her mouth and I see braces, I think I might have given her too many years with my first guess.

"Hi, welcome to Comfort Food! I'm Hannah," she says with such enthusiasm that I question if she's going to leap over the table and sit down with us.

"It's great to have you here. Here are menus, and let's get you started on some drinks."

My cousin looks up at her like he can't open his eyes wide enough and says, "I'll have a Coke, Hannah."

"Make that two," I mumble as I let my gaze slide over the plastic coated menu.

"Got it! Two Cokes. I'll be right back, but I wanted to mention that our sandwich of the day is a grilled cheese with tomato and herb mayonnaise. Be right back!"

I lift my eyes from the menu to watch her ass in her too-tight shorts as she walks away. Interesting place. Diner décor with a touch of Hooters.

"That grilled cheese sounds good," Alex says, sounding a little too peppy for my taste.

"Is that girl rubbing off on you? She was only here

for a minute, at most, and now you sound as up as her. Or is it the shorts and white T-shirt that's got you all excited?" I ask, still reading the menu of more fried and greasy foods than I've ever seen in my life.

He doesn't answer, but I know him well enough after all these years, so I lift my head and see him glaring across the table at me. "You know what your problem is? You're a snob, Cade. Comes from going to that school up north."

His insult misses its mark entirely, especially coming from him. "You're the guy who calls everyone who owns a goddamned spatula a chef, and you work in a five star restaurant, for God's sake. You went to school for culinary arts, and I'm a snob?"

That little bit of truth stops him cold, so he twists his face into a sneer and says, "Just give this place a chance. You never know. It could be great."

As much as busting my best friend's balls is something I enjoy, I don't say anything back to him. After another quick glance at the menu, I look around for any sign of our server and those drinks she promised to bring right back. She's nowhere to be found, but in the window of one of doors leading to the kitchen, I spy a woman staring out at our table. I only see her for a split second before she disappears.

Too bad. I was hoping to get her attention so maybe she could send over Hannah.

CHAPTER TWO

ade

By the time Hannah finally brings out my hamburger and fries and Alex's turkey club sandwich with fries, I've caught the person in the kitchen staring out at us three times. She disappears every time she realizes I see her, and as much as I doubt anything as exciting as a mystery is occurring at Comfort Food, I can't help but wonder why she keeps looking out at us.

Then it dawns on me. She knows Alex. She probably worked with him at the restaurant at some point, and now she's working here. Maybe she's embarrassed since this place is nothing compared to CK, or maybe she thinks it might be him but she isn't sure.

So much for the latest episode of Diner Mystery Theater.

Alex points at the last bite of my hamburger left on my plate and nods. "See? I told you this would be good. Tell me you didn't love that burger."

As much as I hate to admit it, I loved the burger. In fact, I loved the fries too. I don't want to give him a reason to gloat, though, so I merely shrug. "It's a decent burger. Jeez, Alex. You sound like you're trying to sell this place. I'm not in the market for a diner, thank you."

He finishes his club sandwich and sits back, shaking his head. "I'm not trying to sell anything. I did hear the desserts are the best in the area, though, so we have to try them."

"Quite the hard on for cupcakes, huh? You need to go out more, man. You're starting to turn into some deranged version of that celebrity chef dude I watched the other night."

"Whatever. Don't try the desserts. Be a grumpy guy who refuses to enjoy anything," he grumbles under his breath.

Times like this show how different the two of us are. Alex is all about the senses. He gets off on how good things taste or feel. The chef in him talks about how things are presented, like that's a big deal.

I, on the other hand, am not as much a hedonist as he is. Oh sure, I indulge in almost anything that makes me feel good, but he takes it to places I never would. Like desserts. I can't remember the last time I had a dessert. Maybe my grandmother's birthday party last year? She had a cake, which Alex talked about like it was the goddamned Taj Mahal of food, so maybe then?

But he's my best friend and practically my brother, so I accept how he is. Born three months after me, we basically grew up together. For the past twenty-three years, other than my time in college, we hung out every day. I'm closer to him than anyone else in the world.

"I guess I could try something. Maybe they have some kind of doughnut I'd like."

Alex shakes his head and laughs. "You give me a hard time about stopping here because it's a diner, but you want a doughnut?"

"Don't bash the doughnut. It's the breakfast of champions."

"The person who makes the desserts is an artist. I don't think she makes doughnuts."

Now it's my time to do an eye roll. "An arteest?" I say, making sure he understands how utterly ridiculous I think he sounds about all of this.

Before he can give me a hard time about not taking this whole pastry chef and their desserts seriously enough, a man stops at our table. I look up to see him smiling as he notices our empty plates.

He points at them and says, "I hope this means you enjoyed your meals."

Quickly, Alex shoots me a nasty glance and smiles back at the man. "They were great. Best club sandwich I've had in a while."

As they talk about the turkey and something about the lettuce tasting some particular way, I glance past the man and see the woman in the window again. For the first time, I smile. She doesn't smile back, and after looking panicked that I noticed her, she disappears once more.

Strange.

"I'm dying to see what desserts you have today, Robert. I've heard great things about them," Alex says, practically gushing about these fucking desserts again.

What the hell has he heard about these cakes? Now he's on a first-name basis with this guy too?

Robert walks away to check what they have, but he returns a few seconds later looking all long-faced. "I don't see any. Let me check in the back to see if there'll be any ready soon."

"I'd love the chance to meet your pastry chef. I work as a chef at CK," Alex says with a smile.

"Oh, I wish I could, but I can't let anyone back there because she's very particular about her work."

Alex nods. "I completely understand. Trust me. I do. I wouldn't want strangers loping through my kitchen either."

"Let me go check to see what she has. I'll be right back."

After he walks away, I nudge Alex's forearm. "So the pastry chef is particular? Here? Sounds like bullshit to me."

"She's an artist, Cade. You don't fuck around with an artist's area. I get it."

"Well, I don't. This sounds utterly pretentious. Dare I say, snobbish?"

Alex shakes his head. "You don't get it. I do. She has a space where she creates things. Having people she doesn't know in that space affects her."

"Can we leave yet, or are we sticking around for some cake or pie we could get anywhere else on the damn planet? I have things to do."

"You have nothing to do that can't be pushed off for an hour more. Whoever she is, she can wait."

That he assumes it's a woman that's making me want to leave here is a logical guess but an incorrect one. Since I don't want to start a discussion about my love life, I sit back and let out a huff of disgust.

All of this for something that isn't even a doughnut.

Out of the corner of my eye, I see one of the kitchen doors open, and there in full view for me is the woman who's been peering out the window at us for the last half hour. In her arms, she carries a tray of what look like cookies, but I barely waste a second studying them since she's stunning.

Is this the famous pastry chef my cousin can't talk enough about?

I barely get enough time to see she has light blond hair that goes to just below her shoulders and blue eyes. She looks like one of those stunning girls that hang out at the beach, not someone who spends her days in a kitchen.

When she sees I'm looking at her, she hurries back behind those doors, but now she doesn't sneak any peeks out at me. Disappointed, I look across the table at Alex and see by the look on his face he noticed her too.

"Is that her? The person who makes the desserts?" I ask, suddenly curious about these tasty treats he can't talk enough about.

"I don't know, but damn, whoever she is, she's gorgeous. I got the feeling she liked what you looked like," he says with a chuckle.

"She's been looking out at us the whole time we've been here. I figured she knew you from the restaurant. You know, since you both work in the same business."

Shaking his head, he laughs again. "Trust me, if anyone who looked like that worked at CK, I'd know. Kane's been doing the hiring for the past few months, and I swear to God the guy won't even consider someone to work in the kitchen who doesn't have ten years' experience under their belt. That pretty much ensures everyone, male and female, is in their forties, at least."

"Thank God for nepotism, right?" I say, taking this one opportunity to bust his balls.

He shrugs off my jab at how he got his job. "I guess, but that means I don't get to work with anyone even close to my age."

I look around for the mystery woman and don't see her. "So what do you know about this pastry chef?"

"Suddenly interested?" he asks with a chuckle.

"I'm not dead, man. I'm just jaded and a snob, remember? But even someone like that can appreciate a woman that gorgeous."

Robert returns a few moments later and blocks my

view of the kitchen doors. "These are the creations for today. Hailey calls them lace cookies."

He sets a plate with a cookie down in front of each of us. "I hope you enjoy them."

I want to ask him more about this Hailey, but he hurries away before I can get a word out. Alex stares down in awe at the rectangle cookie that looks like white lace over a dark chocolate dough.

"Look at these scalloped edges and what she's done with the icing. It looks like actual lace. What did I tell you? Artist. That's the only word for the person who can create something like this. I need to get a picture of these."

As much as I don't usually go all crazy for cookies, I can't disagree with what he's saying. I've never seen anything that looks like this cookie in front of me. The icing truly does look like real lace, and not just some basic design. What look like delicate flowers and leaves made out of icing sit on top of this dark cookie, and I'm not even sure I should eat something so beautiful.

Alex doesn't have that issue, though, and once he gets finished taking half a dozen pictures of his cookie, his hedonistic ways take over. With one bite, he looks like he's in heaven. His eyes roll back in his head, making him look like he's about to get off right here in the booth.

"It tastes even better than it looks, Cade. Holy fuck, you have to try this cookie. It's chocolate but not like anything I've ever tasted before."

Lifting it to my mouth to take a bite, I joke, "You

going to be okay over there? We need to leave this place sometime soon, so try to tamp down the hard on you've got going on."

One taste of that cookie when it hits my tongue and I know why he's acting like he is. It's delicious. Actually, that isn't a good enough word for it, but I don't know what would be good enough to explain how sweet and light it tastes at the same time.

When Robert returns wearing a hopeful look, I don't give Alex a chance to talk and say, "I'd love to meet the person who made this. It's incredible."

Alex immediately joins in on the praise. "They are fantastic. From one chef to another, I'd be honored if we could tell her how wonderful we think they are."

Robert seems to hesitate for a moment but then nods, giving us a smile like he's proud of his pastry chef. "Okay. I'll get her."

The two of us wait, and Alex says in a low voice, "Try not to be your usual dick self. She might actually like you if you aren't."

Nice. My best friend thinks I'm a dick. And a snob.

I consider asking him what the hell that comment means, but before I can, Robert returns with the person I'm silently calling the woman of my dreams. A couple yards away before, she looked stunning. Up close, she's even better.

Twice in the span of a few minutes, I don't have the right word to describe something regarding her.

"Gentlemen, this is Hailey, my daughter. She's the

one who makes the wonderful desserts for our restaurant," Robert says, beaming pride.

Hailey. At least now I officially know the name of the woman of my dreams. The problem is my dream woman isn't even looking up at me. Not that she's looking at Alex either. In fact, her gaze seems plastered to the floor.

"I'm Cade, and this is Alex. We loved what you made. It's delicious."

Finally, she lifts her head and gives me a tiny smile before glancing over at Alex. "My father told me you're a chef and you loved the cookie? That's so nice of you to say."

Alex's face lights up at her mention of his job. "I am, and I can say for certain I've never tasted anything as incredible from any of our pastry chefs at CK. Just don't tell them I said that because they'll never let me live that down."

Unlike with me, Hailey gives him a big smile that shows off a beautiful mouth and white teeth. "Thank you so much. I really appreciate it."

She gives me a quick glance and then quietly says, "It was nice meeting you two. I have to get back to work now."

And with that, she hurries into the kitchen and the last thing I see is the back of her right before the doors swing closed and she disappears. Robert and Alex continue to talk about desserts and how talented Hailey is, but I can't take my eyes off those kitchen doors, hoping for one more glimpse of her.

She doesn't appear, though, and when her father

walks away and Alex starts talking about how much the check is compared to how great the food was, I simply nod my agreement. I can't think of anything but Hailey.

Is she cool like that with everyone? No, it's obvious she isn't. She didn't act all chilly with Alex.

Is she just shy? Maybe. I can work with shy. Shy girls are some of the sexiest girls going.

Or is she just not interested? Or worse, interested in my best friend?

"Did you hear me? I said I'm going to pay the bill."

Alex's voice pulls me from my thoughts, and I give him a fake smile and nod again. "Yeah. I'll be right there."

Left alone, I look over at the kitchen doors one last time and see her face in the window. This time, she doesn't immediately run and hide. I notice she doesn't look over toward where Alex was sitting either.

When she gives me a tiny smile like she gave me before, I give her one in return. So she's a shy girl. I can definitely work with that.

CHAPTER THREE

$\mathcal{H}$ailey

I HEAR MY MOTHER WALK IN THROUGH THE BACK door of the restaurant and know she's going to come right over to see what I'm making. She means well. Really, she does. It's just that at this very moment the last thing on my mind are cookies.

Shaking my head, I try to push out the image of that guy. Cade. A guy that gorgeous has no business being in our restaurant. Either does his friend, especially since he works as a chef at the best restaurant in town, but I could tell by the way he was talking about the cookie he had that he really liked it.

"Hello, honey," my mother says as she leans over my back to kiss my right cheek. "What do you have cooking today?"

It's her way of being sweet and asking me how I'm

doing. When I was little and Comfort Food was new, she would always say, "Hey, good looking! What you got cooking?" every time she came home from working here.

Back then, I loved when she said that to me. Now when she asks what I'm making, all I feel is anxious. I want these cookies to be as wonderful as they can be so my parents' restaurant does better business, but so far, all they've attracted are over-the-top food bloggers who write long-winded posts that don't get to the point until ten paragraphs in. I can't imagine most people are that patient to wade through all that chatter to find out about my cookies, even if they do include pictures that make them appear even better than they do in person.

I look back at her and give a smile I know she needs to see. "Just a little lace cookie thing I wanted to try. Chocolate shortbread cookies with lace designs on top. Daddy already took them out to the case if you want to see them."

Her blue eyes get big, lighting up at my description. "Oooooh, that sounds incredible! I'm going to go take a look right now. Do you need anything, honey?"

"No, I'm good, Mom. Thanks."

Hearing I'm fine, she runs off to see my latest creations. I hope she doesn't notice how empty the restaurant looks today and focuses only on the cookies.

No sooner does she leave to go out front, she returns with one of the cookies in her hand. "You could be working somewhere incredible, honey. That's how good this is. I wish you'd consider it. Your talents are going to waste here at the diner."

"I'm not interested, Mom. I do this because it makes me happy. I like working here with you and Daddy."

She takes another bite and gives me a sigh like she's in heaven with how good it tastes. "I know, but you're young. You could be out working at somewhere great and meeting people instead of staying in this kitchen every day."

I glance over at the cook at the grill and give him a smile. "I'm sure Hector loves to hear you say that."

A hint of regret fills my mother's eyes. "He knows what I mean." Turning toward him, she yells across the kitchen, "You know I meant no harm, right, Hector?"

My mother couldn't willingly hurt a soul, so he just nods and smiles. He has no interest in getting involved in this conversation. I don't really want to have it either. It seems like lately, that's all my mother wants to talk about with me.

Working somewhere great and meeting new people. I know what she means, even if she doesn't say it.

She means meeting men.

My mother is nothing if not old-fashioned. The time period the diner is meant to simulate would have fit her perfectly. That she was born long after the fifties always amazes me, especially when she gets talking about how I should find a nice young man and settle down.

Settle down? I'm twenty-four, for God's sake.

"Did you hear anything I said, Hailey?" she asks, pulling me from the thought of my life ending before it actually gets started.

I sheepishly shake my head. "No, sorry. I was off in my own head thinking about this macaron I might want to make," I lie.

"Oh, that sounds delightful. Now as to what I was saying."

Damn. I hoped the macaron idea would have changed the subject. No such luck.

"What do you think about the young men your father told me he introduced you to today?" she asks, hope filling her eyes like it always does when she mentions me meeting that elusive fine young man she wishes for me.

"You sure did get a lot of talking done in the few seconds you were out front, Mom," I say as I begin to set up my area to make some more desserts, already so done with this conversation about those guys from earlier.

Should it be cookies or something else? I saw a lemon tartelette that could be great for a beautiful spring day. Do I have what I need? If not, I'll happily run out so I don't have to stay here in this kitchen and talk about this subject that seems so top of mind for my mother.

"He called me on the phone and told me. Now what did you think of them? He said they raved about today's cookie. He also said they both seemed to be very nice men. What did he say their names were? I can't remember the one, but I think he said the one who's also a chef is named Alex. You two would have a lot in common, Hailey. Did you like him?"

I struggle against my nature to tell her Cade's name because I know if I do, she's going to read something into the fact that I remember it when that means nothing. I remember everything. She knows that. She used to joke that I had a mind like a steel trap, but I know if I even mutter his name, she's going to make it something it isn't.

So I just shrug like none of what happened earlier made any impression on me whatsoever. "They were like any other two guys, Mom. How do you and Dad know they aren't gay? They came in together and I saw them talking and it looked like they were bickering. I'm sorry to tell you, but that might mean they're both taken."

The mere thought that those two handsome young men who would be perfect for me could be gay stops my mother for a long moment, and she stands in front of my dough table with her mouth hanging open. It's like her mind is processing the likelihood that those two fine specimens she'd already had me choosing between could possibly not be available, and with every second that passes, she hates the idea more and more. Her expression morphs from one of shock to one of utter unhappiness.

"Well, your father thought they might be brothers

since they resembled one another," she says, practically snapping at me for ruining her fantasy.

They did look alike. Both had dark brown hair and brown eyes, and they did both have tattoos up and down their arms. It never occurred to me they could be brothers, though, but in all honesty, I only paid attention to the one named Cade, especially once I found out Alex is a chef at a five star restaurant.

I'm not a chef, by any stretch of the imagination, so being around someone who actually is instantly makes me feel self-conscious. A chef at the best restaurant in town? I couldn't have focused on him if I wanted to.

"Well, I have no idea, Mom. It's not like we had a deep conversation or anything. They liked the cookie and told me so. I thanked them and came back here to do work. That was it. If Daddy made it out to be anything else, then he was seeing something I wasn't."

My mother's five foot five body seems to deflate right in front of me at my disinterest in Cade and Alex. "Oh. I just thought since they came in and they were young like you that you might have wanted to get to know them. It's not every day young men come into the diner here, Hailey."

"Sorry. I didn't have my man-hunting thing going on today. Maybe if they come in again."

She grimaces, twisting her face into a disapproving scowl. "You know, honey, it's no crime to like people. You're a beautiful young woman who shouldn't think she should spend all her time hiding away in a kitchen. When opportunity knocks, you want to make sure to answer that door."

I grab the rolling pin from the rack next to me and drop it onto my table. It makes a loud thud that startles my mother.

"Oh, my God, Mom! Opportunity did not knock just because two good looking men came into this restaurant. I don't care if one is a chef or not, and just because he works around food doesn't make us have anything in common. I'm not a chef! There is no comparison to what he does and what I do here. As for the other one, I didn't even catch his name, so I'm sorry to disappoint you, but this episode of Set Up Your Daughter With Hot Strangers has come to an end."

Instantly, I see in her eyes that I've hurt her feelings. Frowning, she gives me a nod and silently turns to leave the kitchen as regret fills me.

"I'm sorry. I didn't mean that. Well, I did, but not that way, Mom."

Without turning around, she nods again. "It's fine, honey. I'm just going to go out front and see how things were this afternoon."

Every word sounds sadder than the last, so by the time she gets to the end of her sentence, I think I hear a tiny sob. Nice going. First, I'm my usual backward self with those two guys, and then I'm my other usual self, the defensive one, with my mother.

Grabbing the dough from the mixing bowl behind me, I slam it onto the table and begin working it. I better get used to working alone here because at the rate I'm going, even Hector is not going to want to be around me.

So much for thinking I'd made so much progress this past year. That was obviously as wrong as wrong can be.

I look up toward the kitchen door, hoping to see my mother come back so I can tell her I didn't mean to hurt her feelings. I understand what she's trying to do. I do. She has that whole mentality of getting back up on the horse after it's thrown you off. It's how she and my father continue to fight to keep this business open year after year long after other people would have given up.

That attitude is to be admired, but love isn't like running a struggling business. Sometimes, a person can't find the will to get back up and dust themselves off after being thrown. Sometimes, it just feels better to stay down where you are on the safe ground.

It's been almost a year since I've been down here, and as much as I thought I was getting back to who I was before it all happened, that was just wishful thinking. I'm still that brokenhearted soul Malcolm threw away that beautiful June night eleven months ago. All the hours spent talking to the therapist have added up to one sad truth.

I'm not ready to get back up on that horse again. I'm still hurting from the last fall.

CHAPTER FOUR

ade

BRIGHT AND EARLY THE NEXT DAY, I HEAD DOWN TO CK to see what I can find out from my uncles about this Hailey person. Unlike Alex, they should know something since they supposedly tried to lure her to CK as a pastry chef.

I find Cassian and Kane both in the office, which is a surprise. I'd have been happy simply trolling for information with one of them. Maybe this is a good sign.

"Hi! It's your favorite nephew come to visit," I say to announce my arrival as I walk into the office the two of them share.

Kane looks up and gives me a big smile. "Hey, what are you doing here? Decide you want to put that business degree to good use finally?"

Cassian just shakes his head. "What's up, Cade?"

I grab a chair on the other side of the room and take a seat. "You sound like my father, Kane. Have you two been meeting to compare notes on how to shanghai me into the club or restaurant business?"

My question makes him laugh. "The last time your father came here to talk to me, we almost got into a fist fight. Trust me, we are not comparing notes on anything."

"Good, because one of him is enough. I don't need two of you trying to convince me what to do with my life."

Kane holds his hands up in front of him like he's surrendering. "No convincing here. But whoever thought it would be Stefan who turned into the dad who wanted his son to figure out life so young?"

Cassian laughs, and I'm tempted to ask exactly what Kane means by that, but I'm not really interested in taking a trip down memory lane with my uncles today. I already know a little about how my father was when he was my age. I can hear more another day.

Right now, I have other topics I want to discuss with them. Other more beautiful and interesting topics.

Might as well jump right in. "So, what do you guys know about the pastry chef over at that restaurant, Comfort Food?"

"We were definitely interested in having her work for us, but she denied us cold. No way. Wouldn't even return our calls, no matter if it was me or Kane."

Interesting. Then again, Comfort Food is her

family's restaurant. She probably feels allegiance to them. But to give up the chance to work at the best restaurant in town to stay at the family diner seems foolish.

"Okay, but what do you know about her?" I ask, hoping to get more than this scratching the surface bullshit.

"For the longest time nobody knew it was even a her," Kane says. "A few local food bloggers got a hold of her treats and asked the owners of the restaurant, but they didn't tell them it was their daughter who made them. Only when the bloggers went snooping around did they find out it was a young woman named Hailey Canton, the daughter of the owners of the restaurant."

"Do you know anything else?"

Kane looks at me like he can't understand why I'd be asking about this woman at all. Clearly, he hasn't seen her.

"Like what? What else is there to know? Have you tasted any of her desserts? It's not an exaggeration to say they're the best most people around here have ever had. That's why we wanted her to come work for us, but she said no. Or more correctly, her father told us she wasn't even interested in talking about it."

"Alex says she's some kind of artist. He was raving about her like she was the Michelangelo of cookies yesterday."

Cassian laughs at his son's over-the-top response to that dessert. "I saw the pics of the cookies she made.

The lace ones. I don't think he was wrong to rave. He told me they were delicious."

"They were," I admit with a shrug. "I mean, as far as cookies go, I guess. So she makes nice cookies. Why does she act like some kind of diva? She wouldn't even talk to either of us yesterday when Alex asked to meet her to compliment her on the cookie. It was weird. Then when she came out, it felt like she didn't even want to bother talking with us."

"Artists are like that, Cade. We've had some chefs who act like her. They're passionate about what they create. You have to give them that," Kane says as he stands from behind his desk.

"Artists. The way you guys talk like these people are DaVinci or something...I don't get it. Does that give people license to act like dicks?"

Both my uncles look at one another and laugh. "Sounds like she got under your skin a little bit. Not used to having women not interested in you?" Cassian asks with a chuckle.

Well, at least I got a little information out of them before they started busting my balls. Leave it to my family. Too bad Olivia and Abbi weren't the ones I could ask about Hailey. They'd give me chapter and verse, every detail from what she does in her spare time to how long she's been single.

Or maybe she's not single. Is that why she was so cool yesterday?

No, that doesn't work because she was fine with Alex.

I stand from my chair and push it back against the

wall where I got it from. "Well, thanks guys. I better get going."

As I turn to walk toward the door, Cassian asks, "Why do you want to know about this pastry chef?"

His tone says he knows exactly why I want to know about her. Alex probably told him everything that happened yesterday.

When I don't answer his question, Kane chuckles. "Alex told us what she looks like, Cade. Guess the whole diva thing isn't that much of a turn off."

I look back over my shoulder and throw him a cocky smile. "I'm not against a challenge."

"Oh yeah? Turn over a new leaf or something?"

He's not wrong mocking me on that. I do have a history that indicates the exact opposite of liking a challenge when it comes to women. I'll admit that.

But something about Hailey makes me think I might be interested in one with her.

"I actually like the idea of having to work through whatever she has going on. Personally, I'm not sure it's not a shy thing instead of a diva thing, and if that's the case, I'm all in."

My uncles look at one another in disbelief. So maybe my history more than indicates challenging women haven't been my thing. Fine. A guy can change, can't he?

"You know what they say about shy girls, don't you?" I ask them.

Kane stares at me blankly, and Cassian shrugs. "No idea."

I shake my head at the state of the two men I

thought were the coolest guys in the world growing up. "You two need to get out of this office more. Seriously."

"Well, I'm wondering if you aren't aiming above your level, Cade. Alex couldn't say enough about how gorgeous she is. Good looking and talented? Maybe she was cool because she's just not into you," Kane says with a laugh.

"Yeah. I mean, she might have told you everything you need to know yesterday. You just don't want to see it," Cassian adds.

Before they have a chance to bust my balls about trying to date out of my sphere, I head toward the back door of CK. Leave it to family to act like I'm the one who can't get her and not vice versa.

So she's beautiful and talented? So what? I'm not exactly some loser walking around without any skills here. True, I don't have my entire life planned out like nearly everyone else in my family. It's not because I can't do that.

It's because I won't.

Anyway, what woman wants a guy who's all settled down at the age of twenty-three? Women want excitement and fun, and that's what I offer in spades.

Leave that life all planned out shit for guys as old as my uncles. I'm way too young to be dealing with that yet.

And I'm betting that Hailey is a woman who could use some excitement in her life.

ailey

POKING MY HEAD INTO THE KITCHEN, I GIVE MY
father a smile. "Hey, what's new?"

He shakes his head and sighs. "What's new is it's
your day off. You don't have to be here every day,
honey. You made more than enough desserts
yesterday, so why don't you go out and enjoy yourself
on such a beautiful day?"

"Coming through!" Ginger announces as she
practically barrels through the kitchen doors, nearly
taking me with her.

I quickly step out of the way so the doors don't
come back and slam into my face. After a few seconds,
I walk back to where my father is working near my
area and answer his question.

"Don't worry. I'm not here for long. I just wanted

to see how the lemon tartelettes did, and it seems they went over pretty big. There are only a few left, and it's only two o'clock in the afternoon. Did one of those food bloggers post about them and that's why people came in to grab them?"

He gives me his usual confused look that he always wears when I start talking about the food bloggers. My father simply doesn't understand why anyone would write about my desserts like they do. When they first started featuring my creations, he read a few of their posts and complained the entire time that they said almost nothing about the restaurant or how good my desserts are but instead talked about their childhoods the whole time.

I tried to explain that's how they do it, but he wouldn't listen. Since then, whenever I mention them, he looks at me like I've switched from English to Greek and he doesn't comprehend a word I'm saying.

It's the same look he used to get when I was a teenager and had a crush on a boy. He didn't want to understand I was growing up then, and he doesn't want to understand those food bloggers and their posts now.

So instead of discussing them, he switches to business mode. "We had a bit of a lunch rush pretty early for midweek. It started even before eleven, and it just ended a few minutes ago. I mentioned the dessert of the day, which is what I'm calling them now, to a few people, and from there they took off."

"I'm so happy to hear that! Anyone new seem to come in?" I ask, more curious about if what I'm

34

making is bringing new customers in than if the tartelettes were a hit with the regulars.

In his stoic way, he nods and thinks about the question for a moment. "Maybe. I thought I saw a couple new people today. But you don't need to shoulder the responsibility for bringing new people into the restaurant, Hailey. We're fine with the customers we have right now."

The two of us know that's a lie, but I don't let him see I know the truth. My father is a proud man, and I would never want to hurt him like that.

It doesn't change the fact that I hope my desserts help people find this place and make it a go-to restaurant for them in the future. He doesn't have to know that, though.

"Well, I'm going to get out of here then. It is a beautiful day, so I thought I'd get a little Vitamin D and then catch up with Meadow after her big job interview. She's meeting with the owners of the biggest design firm in town right now."

My father's face brightens at the mention of my best friend. "Tell her we said hi and that we hope she gets the big job. If she does, you have to go out and celebrate."

I know what he's doing. My mother has rubbed off on him and now he's slyly trying to get me to go out more. He's just not as obvious about it.

"We will. Don't worry. You know Meadow. If there's a chance to celebrate, she's there. She'd celebrate days ending in y if she had the time," I joke before waving goodbye to him. "See you tomorrow, Dad."

"Have fun getting your vitamins!" he calls after me, thinking he's funny.

I do have to admit it, though. He is cute when he tries to be amusing.

On my way out the front door of the restaurant, I give Ginger a smile, which she doesn't return. She saves the niceties for the customers. That's good, I guess, but it would be nice if she sometimes didn't act like everyone else who works here is a sworn enemy of her family who she must growl or bark at every chance she gets.

Even my parents and I don't get a break from her rudeness, and my family owns this place. But she's good with customers, so she stays, snappy attitude and all.

As I head toward my car, I see a red Jaguar with tinted windows pull into the parking lot. Maybe those food bloggers are helping. It's pretty rare we get that kind of clientele here. Maybe they'll like the lemon tartelettes and tell some of their wealthy friends. That would help my parents.

I watch as the driver's side door opens and see Cade, the guy from the day I made the lace chocolate cookies. My attention switches to the passenger side door while I wait to see if his friend came back with him, but it doesn't open.

He's alone. But why is he here at all? He didn't strike me as the kind of guy who's a big fan of cookies. His friend maybe, but not him.

Unsure what to do, I hurry to my car. I fumble with my keys to get my door open, and while I'm silently wishing I hadn't locked the damn doors in the first place since it's the middle of the day and I'm at my family's restaurant, I hear footsteps behind me.

When I turn to look, there he is coming toward my car. What does he want to talk to me about? We don't know one another. I barely spoke to him the other day.

God, he's good looking. Like the kind of good looking that makes you wonder if he's real. Men like that don't tend to come looking for women like me. So what is he doing walking this way?

Maybe he is a guy who loves cookies. Too bad I have to tell him all we have are tartelettes today.

"Hey, Hailey? How are you?"

I stop dead and slowly turn my entire body around to face him. Jesus, up close he's even better. I didn't think he was this good looking the other day. Then again, I spent most of my time looking at him through the dingy kitchen door window and barely made eye contact with him when I went to his table.

He's wearing a light blue T-shirt and a pair of jeans, but I swear I've never seen anyone look this good in clothes like that before. It's got to be the muscles. He looks like he works out.

That's what he is. A gym rat. But a gym rat who cheats by eating sugary desserts? That doesn't sound right. Or maybe it is. I don't exactly have a wealth of knowledge about that kind of man.

All of this runs through my head as I stand there staring at him and then realize I haven't answered him.

How am I? Not good, Cade. A nervous wreck would be the appropriate description, I think.

"Hi. What are you doing here?" I ask, knowing how rude that must sound, like I've been taking nasty lessons from Ginger. But I can't help but be curious at what's brought him back for the second time in a week to a restaurant he's never been to before the other day.

"I came to see you."

The way he says that, as if it's the only answer and I should know that, makes me even more nervous. He's way too confident. That I can tell already.

He smiles, and I think my insides begin to melt. I'm like chocolate morsels in the sun looking at that sexy grin. Oh, yeah. Way too confident. I bet women really like that smile.

Then again, why wouldn't they? Nice teeth. White. Straight. What's not to like?

Out of nowhere, my brain switches into idiot mode, and I ask, "Do you mean you came to see me because of the cookies?"

Cade looks confused for a moment but shakes his head. "Not really."

"Because I didn't make any today. It's my day off. I made a different dessert yesterday, though, and if you love lemon, you should definitely go in and check it out."

"I didn't come here for food."

Now I feel foolish and uncomfortable, so I blurt out something I know is a lie. "Oh, because I thought you and your friend might be food bloggers. Some of the local ones have been doing write-ups about what I make."

He smiles and shakes his head again. "No. My friend is actually my cousin. Alex is a chef like you. I do nothing with food other than eat it. That I'm very talented at."

I can't help but let my gaze roam down his muscular, toned body as I decide he's a liar like I am. Or maybe he just eats really healthy stuff to get to look like that.

When I don't say anything to what I'm sure can't be the truth, he says, "So it's your day off? Want to go do something?"

"You mean you and me? Us do something?"

"Yeah," he says and then chuckles. "I thought maybe we could hang out and get to know one another. I saw you looking through the window at me the other day. It's fine that you're shy. I have enough confidence for both of us."

"It seems like you do."

"That's not a bad thing, though. I mean, the shyness. I like that. I bet once you get to know someone you aren't so quiet anyway, so I thought we could start on getting to know one another today."

"Are you always like this with women?" I ask, unsure if I'm put off by how forward he is or intrigued that he truly is this confident.

"I don't hesitate when I see someone I like. I think you like me too. I mean, unless you were checking out Alex the other day, but I didn't get the feeling you were. You seemed more interested in me," he says in that smooth way that seems so natural to him.

Hearing he likes me makes every ounce of anxiety that lives inside me rear its ugly head. I should have never looked out that kitchen window at him. That's what I get for listening to Dr. Thorpe and Meadow.

Put yourself out there, Hailey. Let people know you like them. Try it.

This is what happens when I take their advice. I end up in a parking lot talking to some gorgeous guy and feeling like the only thing I want to do is run away before I say or do something so utterly ridiculous that I humiliate myself.

Looking down at my keys I'm gripping tightly in my hand, I mumble, "I have to go. You should go inside and have one of the lemon desserts I made. You might like them."

And then before he can say another word, possibly that it was a mistake to come here today because I'm just a basket case, I run inside the restaurant and hide in the kitchen back near my station.

Ten minutes later, after pretending like I was looking for something just in case someone saw me tear back here, I look out that same kitchen door window where he saw me checking him out the other day and see there's no red Jaguar in the parking lot. For a moment, relief washes over me, but then that's replaced by regret, like always when I push people away like I just did with Cade.

I sneak out the back door of the restaurant this time and walk out to my car, silently berating myself for being exactly who I swore I wouldn't be anymore. But if you're not ready, you're not ready. It doesn't matter what the horse looks like or that he likes you.

By the time I reach my car, I can't remember what I wanted to do today because all I want to do now is go home and crawl underneath the covers. As I slide into the driver's seat, a white piece of paper stuck under one of my windshield wipers flaps in the breeze. When I grab it and open it up, I see it's from Cade.

Hey, give me a call sometime. I think we could have fun. I promise I don't bite. Unless you want me to. 555-2466

Cade March

Quickly, I stuff the note into my pocket and decide right there and then there's no way I'm ever going to call him. I may be afraid to get back on the dating horse, but some people you should be afraid of.

Men like Cade March.

CHAPTER SIX

ade

AFTER CHECKING MY PHONE FOR THE FIFTH TIME, I toss it onto the other side of the bed in disgust. She got my note. I'm sure of it. So why hasn't she called? It's been almost twenty-four hours.

Maybe this arteest isn't for me.

Bullshit. She and I could be having a good time if only she'd call. I should have stuck around to get her number, but after watching her run away into the restaurant, I can't be blamed for calling an audible. It's not every day a woman flees from me like she's running from a house fire.

She'll call. They always do. And why not? Who doesn't want to have a good time?

I close my eyes and ease my palm over my cock. Just thinking about her gets me hard. I can only imagine how incredible it's going to feel to actually kiss her. After that, it's all good from there.

And then in the middle of my daydream about how fucking fantastic it's going to be with Hailey, I hear a voice I know all too well call out my name. Thanks for crashing my fantasy, Dad.

"Cade? Where are you? It's the middle of the day."

I know damn well what time it is. Why does he have to do his Big Ben impression for me this afternoon?

Quickly, I get into a pair of shorts and scrub the remnants of last night's sleep from my face before heading out into my living room. There, standing in the middle next to the coffee table, my father swivels his head left and right examining the room like he's never seen the place before.

"Hey, Dad. How did you get in?"

It's a valid question, if not a polite one. I'm all for family togetherness, but just walking up into my condo and interrupting what was going to be a fine jerk off session is a bridge too far.

"You left the door open. Pretty trusting, don't you think?" he says with all the disapproval he can fit into those few words.

"Not trusting. Forgetful. I thought I locked it when I went to bed," I say before turning to walk toward the kitchen. "Can I get you anything, Dad?"

"No, not unless it's juice. Your mother has me on this juice cleanse for the next two days. I think she might be trying to kill me."

I look back at him and see in his expression he's

serious. "She's not trying to kill you. She's just trying to make you healthier. I might have orange juice, but I can't promise it's still good. Someone left it after the party a couple weekends ago."

He follows behind, begging off the possibly rancid juice that's sitting in the back of my refrigerator. "I'm good. I'm thinking I might just stick with water until this whole cleanse thing is up. Water has to be better for you than juice."

I grab a bottle of spring water and hand it over the refrigerator door to him. "It might be, but it doesn't have the vitamins and nutrients juice has."

My father thinks about that for a moment and smiles. "Don't tell your mother then. I just know I can't drink another glass of carrot juice or I'm going to turn into a rabbit. Does my skin look orange to you? Someone at the club said I was looking a little orange and asked if I went heavy on the self-tanner. As if I'd use that shit. If I didn't need all the bartenders I could find, I'd fire that little shit Antonio. Asshole."

My father's stream of consciousness makes me laugh. One second he's talking about turning into a rabbit, and the next he's threatening one of his bartenders.

"So what can I do for you, Dad? I'm guessing it's important since you didn't bother to even knock before you came in."

"It's not like I broke in, Cade. The door was unlocked, so I walked in."

Why this sounds right to him I have no idea. It's

not like I'm still a kid living in his house and he found my bedroom door unlocked.

"Yeah, you said. Do you routinely check to see if people's front doors are unlocked when you go to someone's house?" I ask as I take my place across the kitchen from him and lean back against the countertop.

His expression hardens into a grimace. "You aren't someone. You're my son."

Somewhere in there I sense there's a sentiment I should be unhappy with, but there's no point in getting into it with my father today. He's just being his usual dad self.

"Got it. So what's up?"

He looks around my kitchen that could use some cleaning and sighs. Okay, maybe it could use a sandblasting to dislodge the crusty food stuck on the stove. And the countertops.

"So, is this what you're planning to do today? Just hang around?" he asks before wincing, like my condo is causing him some terrible pain.

I can't help but get defensive when he does this. It's not like it's rare that this happens either. Lately, it seems like at least once a month, he drops in and examines my place like some kind of disgruntled housekeeper come to heap shame on someone for not keeping it tidy enough.

"Well, I wasn't even up when you barged in, Dad, so I'd say I've accomplished a few things already today," I snap back, all the while smiling because I really don't need to get into an argument with my father not a half hour after waking up.

More wincing is followed by him silently taking a drink of water while I wait for the inevitable discussion that's going to occur. I know my father too well to believe he's going to be able to leave here without giving me the lecture about how it's time for me to grow up and settle down.

At twenty-three.

It's the height of hypocrisy too, if you ask me. I've heard the stories of how legendary his twenties were working at Club X and living a life others could only dream about. Money, women, and all the alcohol he could want was his everyday life.

Yet I'm expected to be settled down into a responsible life at my age.

"Do you have any job prospects, Cade? It's been a year since you graduated from college. You have a degree, you're a smart guy, and I have to think there are hundreds of companies that would love to have you work for them."

As he speaks, I anticipate every word that will come out of his mouth next. I've heard this speech so many times, I could give it to myself. That would actually be better. It would cut out the middle man and make having to do this with him a thing of the past.

That wouldn't work for the great Stefan March, though. No, he enjoys coming over here on his monthly tour of my house, sighing disapprovingly as he scans the rooms and mentally ticks off all my household failures, and then giving me his same old dissertation on how I should be working at a job he would have never considered at my age and likely wouldn't even now.

"Dad, you know the answer, so why do you ask the question? I haven't found what I want to do yet. I have time. It's not like being twenty-three and unsure of my future makes me a lost cause. I have money, so I'm not going to be homeless anytime soon. Don't worry. I got this."

My father narrows his eyes like he can't believe what I'm saying. "You got what, Cade?"

I spread my arms out and smile. "This. Life."

"You've got a condo because of your trust fund your mother and I set up. You've got that car of yours because of that same trust fund. Don't you think it's time to make your own way in life?"

"I am. I'm just not doing it the way you would prescribe for me."

He acts like that trust fund isn't exactly like the money he got from his father all those years ago that allowed him and his brothers to start up Club X. Fuck, he's such a hypocrite!

Taking a step forward, he lets out another frustrated sigh and sets his water bottle on the island that separates us. "Cade, you have the very skills necessary to take over the club. You'd be perfect. I'm not going to be running it forever, and it's turnkey. Literally, you'd walk in and it would set you up for life. Then you could do whatever you want with it. Change it to be exactly what you want it to be. It's there for the taking."

And there's the pitch that comes right near the end of every one of these monthly discussions. Now it's my turn to say that's not what I want to do and his turn to get angry, throw his hands up in the air, and storm out.

At least all of this is predictable. I have to give him that.

"Dad, I don't want to manage a club or own a club or do anything with your club. It's not who I am."

Right on cue, disappointment fills his dark eyes and he lowers his head to look at the floor. "Your mother and I always thought we were doing right by you when we set up that trust fund to begin paying out when you were twenty-one. We wanted to make sure we took care of the future because we love you, son."

He stops for a moment and looks up at me with anguish written all over his face. This isn't how our usual talks go. Why isn't he raging like always? This is when he's supposed to list all the ways I should be acting like an adult and how I should have some job that he approves of by now.

But that doesn't seem to be happening this time. Interesting. My father has changed things up on me.

"We see now we made a mistake, and we intend on rectifying that. From this year on, the payments won't occur unless you have a job. We don't care if it's flipping burgers or delivering pizzas. A job is a job, and as long as you're doing an honest day's work and you're happy doing it, we'll be happy for you."

I stand there in my kitchen staring at him, stunned at what he's just said. "You're taking my trust fund away from me?"

"No, Cade. You will, if you don't get a job. Again, your mother and I don't care what you choose to do, as long as it's legal and you earn money doing it. We put no restrictions whatsoever on you. Now, if you want, you can work at the club and this will be solved. I always need bartenders, and since you have no interest in managing the club, maybe you'd like to do a job that's less work and more fun. It's entirely up to you."

Barely able to contain my anger at this blackmail he's decided to use on me, I snap, "So as long as I work behind the bar serving those goddamned drunks you call customers, you won't cut me off? Nice, Dad. Hell of a way to treat your only son."

He takes a sip of water and smiles. He's won, so why not? "The choice is up to you. You can start whenever you want. Or not. If you want to do something else, do it. If you want to start up a business and make things, do it. If you want to deliver those pizzas or flip those burgers I mentioned before, do it. Just do something, for Christ's sake, Cade!"

And there's the anger I'm used to in our lovely talks. At least he didn't disappoint me with that.

As he's leaving, I quietly give him what he wants. "I'll do some bartending at the club starting this week."

My father doesn't say a word before walking out of the kitchen. From the other room, I hear him say, "Afternoon, Alex. Your cousin is in there. How are things going?"

Sounding as happy as a clam, Alex answers, "Great, Stefan! Nice seeing you. Have a good one!"

By the time he pokes his head around the wall, it's all I can do to force myself to say hi. "You just missed a delightful conversation with my father, the wonderful and hypocritical Stefan March."

A look of pain comes over my cousin's face. "Was it that day already this month? I thought those talks came later in the month and not so early. So did it go the same as always?"

I shake my head, still amazed at what he pulled on me. "No. Daddy's got a brand new routine, and it's utter bullshit."

ade

ALEX WAITS TO HEAR WHAT I MEAN BY THAT AND finally says, "A brand new routine? What does that mean?"

"Seems I'm not going to get any money this year from my trust if I don't get a job."

As much as I wish Alex would be supportive on this, I can see by the look on his face and the shrug he gives to my announcement that he either isn't surprised or may even think what my father's doing is cool.

"Thanks for being there for me, man."

"Cade, I'm your best friend, but even I can say it's time you stopped playing around. You've been back from school for almost a year. You can't be surprised he and your mother pulled this card on you."

Huffing my disgust at that little nugget of truth coming from Alex, of all people, I head over to the refrigerator and grab the two of us beers. I hand him his and push past him on my way to the living room.

At least I can enjoy a couple more days of freedom before I get chained to the workaday world. Leaning back, I close my eyes and take a sip of ice cold beer while the realization that I haven't even had breakfast yet runs through my head.

Oh well. Forget doughnuts. Beer is now the breakfast of champions.

"Come on, Cade. It's not so bad. I work, and it hasn't made me some uptight pain in the ass who doesn't have fun. As my father likes to say, the world is your oyster. You can work at any number of jobs. Just find something you like and do it."

I look across the room to see he's serious about this. "The world is my oyster? Dude. And you've always been a pain in the ass. You working at your job has nothing to do with that."

"Fuck you too," he says with a chuckle, lifting his beer in the air. "To Cade finally joining the ranks of us working stiffs."

That toast sucks, but I take a drink of my beer anyway. "What kills me is he was even worse than me at this age. Remember hearing the stories your father and Kane were telling a few summers ago at the Fourth of July party about my father? To hear them talk, Stefan March spent all his days sleeping and all his nights partying. So that was okay for him, but now he's older so he wants to make sure I don't have any fun? He acts like responsibility is some wonderful thing and having a job is the mark of a good person. What a fraud he is."

Alex nods, even though I have a feeling he agrees with my father at least a little. "By the way they were talking, all three of them were living the life. I guess time changes you, though. We'll probably be that way when we get to be their age."

I couldn't be more horrified at that prospect than if he had the power to show me the future himself. "No. Fucking. Way. I'm not going to turn into that. No, thanks."

"So what kind of job are you thinking you might want? You have a degree in business from a good school, so it's not like you're not qualified for a lot."

Just the thought of what job I might want to get makes my head hurt. If I knew what I wanted to do this past year, I would have done it. While I make it seem like I'm all about living the life of leisure and enjoying myself, even to my best friend, the truth is I don't want to do any job.

Not because I don't want to work. Work is work. If you hate what you're doing, it feels like a jail sentence. If you love what you're doing, time flies. I got through four years of school just fine, so it's not that I can't handle work.

I just have no idea what I want to do.

"No clue," I say shaking my head. "How did you know you wanted to be a chef?" I ask, wondering if hearing this story again might help me figure out what I should do.

Alex thinks about it for a few moments before taking a drink of his beer. "I just always did. I grew up hearing all about what was happening at the restaurant and I thought it sounded great. I found out when I started working at CK when I was a teenager that it wasn't as fun as I'd made it out to be, but I knew I wanted to be a chef."

"I have no idea how you work with your father. I spent last summer working at the club with my father, and I don't know how I'm going to do it again now. I told him I'd do some shifts, but I swear to God I hate the idea more than I can put into words."

My misery makes Alex laugh. "It's not that bad for me, actually. My father and Kane don't really hang out in my kitchen, so I only see them when they pop in or when I go into the restaurant after my shift is over. And Kane is my uncle, and you know how he is. I swear there are some nights I don't hear him speak a word to those of us in the kitchen."

I blow the air out of my lungs in frustration. "Too bad I'm not the son of Cassian March or Kane Jackson."

"It's not bad for me, but Cash gets most of the grief from my dad like you do from your father. I'm guessing that's why my brother's going to be a lawyer and not a chef, like me. He never liked hearing about how the kitchen worked, and remember the first time he saw me making a meal? He laughed in my face."

"If only I loved something as much as you love doing what you do. I still don't get the whole loving cooking food, but at least it's something you're passionate about. I have nothing like that."

Alex smiles and gets that look of pure happiness on his face like whenever he talks about his job. "It's an art form. You take something that's a raw material and you create a masterpiece. Even better, people then eat it and gush about how delicious it tastes. I can't imagine doing anything else."

"An arteest, like that Hailey girl, huh? You should be interested in her. You have that whole food thing in common."

"I love how committed she is to making what she creates so beautiful, but she's not my type," he says like he's thought about getting together with her.

From out of nowhere, jealousy rears up in me. That's never happened before when it comes to him. We've dated sisters, friends, cousins—you name it, and never once have I thought he might be a rival for any woman.

But now with Hailey, he seems perfect for her compared to me. They both do that chef thing and they both love food for something other than putting it into their faces and eating. I doubt she'd run away from any conversation with him.

"What do you mean she isn't your type? She's gorgeous, talented, everything a guy could want. Why wouldn't she be your type?"

"I don't date women in the industry," he answers flatly.

What the hell is he talking about?

"Who are you? Some big movie star? You don't

date in the industry? What kind of bullshit is that? I can't count the number of servers you've been with."

Still, he shakes his head with a definite no. "Servers are different. Fellow chefs? Never. You don't want to date someone just like you."

Now he sounds like a diva. I roll my eyes and shake my head at the nonsense coming out of his mouth. "That's ridiculous. I thought having things in common was what you need for a relationship."

He seizes on my use of the word relationship, practically leaping out of the chair when he asks, "So now we're talking about relationships? First you have to get a job, and now you're talking about settling down with someone? I'm guessing you've decided you want Hailey Canton. She's definitely got it all."

Under my breath, I mumble, "Which she ran away with while I tried to talk to her."

Alex leans forward and gives me a strange look. "What did you say?"

He's been my best friend from practically the minute we were born, so I guess I can confess the truth of what happened to him. "I stopped by to talk to her yesterday afternoon. You know, to chat her up and see if she wanted to go for a ride or something."

"No need to explain your methods, Cade. I've seen every move you have. So what happened?"

Blowing the air out between my lips, I sit back in frustration. "Nothing. Well, nothing good. We talked for about five seconds. She sort of looked like she was happy to see me. At least I think she did. Well, after she got over being surprised that I had stopped into that diner again. I asked her if she wanted to hang out, and she said no. She actually thought I had come back for more of those cookies. Wild, huh?"

He hums at the memory of that chocolate lace cookie. Typical Alex. "That cookie was pretty fucking good. She has a gift."

"Yeah, I guess, but I didn't go there to talk about desserts. So I'm trying to talk her up and feel the situation out, and she suddenly said she had to go and ran away. No kidding. She just ran back into the restaurant, even though she was on her way out when I caught up with her. I waited around for a few minutes, but she never came back out. What the hell was that about?"

My cousin's eyes grow wide for a second and then he throws his head back and laughs. "She ran away from you? Dude, you are totally losing your touch. I can't remember a single time a woman has run away from me while I was talking to her. Too funny."

So much for having a best friend you can confide in.

I take a swig of my beer and then chug the rest of it. Slamming the empty bottle on the coffee table, I whip him off. "Fuck you, Alex."

Still laughing, he waves off my irritation. "Okay, my bad. I didn't mean to laugh at your humiliation. You have to remember she's someone who's creative, so maybe she saw your moves coming from a mile away and wasn't having them. Maybe you'll have to do more with this girl than just show up as you with that great car as your calling card."

"Dude, I wasn't standing there in the middle of the Comfort Food parking lot showing her all my moves. I was just trying to have a conversation to get to know her and she…"

I can't bring myself to say she ran away again. I've replayed the scene in my head a hundred times since yesterday, and then every time I checked my phone to see if she texted or called when I was asleep. I may not be the world champion in seducing women, but even I know when one runs away, it's not a good sign.

"She bolted," he says in a serious voice I know is taking every bit of strength he has because he probably wants to continue laughing in my face.

"So what are you going to do? Maybe she's not your type?" Alex asks, giving voice to something I've wondered more than once.

No. I don't know if Hailey is my type, but I want to get to know her before I cross her off my list. Maybe she really is just a shy girl. Nothing wrong with that. I can work with shy.

As long as she doesn't keep running away when I try to talk to her.

"I don't know if she is or isn't, but I'm not ready to throw in the towel quite yet. She's a beautiful woman. I'm me. I don't see why we can't get together and have a good time, right?"

"You're one of a kind, Cade. I can't decide if you're funny or just way too fucking cocky. Either way, you're okay, man. So are we going to sit around talking about your failure with women all day or head out and get this day started? I have to be at work by six, so time's wasting."

He doesn't give me a chance to answer his questions before he grabs my bottle off the table and walks into the kitchen. Alex is one of those creative types. He and Hailey are a lot alike in that way, especially since they both like to create with food. Maybe she's a lot like him, which would be great since he's my best friend.

Sounds like the best of both worlds in one beautiful woman. How could I not take a chance on that?

CHAPTER EIGHT

$\mathscr{H}$ailey

MY PHONE VIBRATES AGAINST MY SIDE, TEARING ME from my thoughts about how I acted with Cade yesterday. I grab it and see it's Meadow calling me. She must want to talk about the interview again, but I'm probably not the best cheerleader at this moment.

"Hey, Meadow! What's up?" I say into the phone as I pretend not to be miserable.

"Hailey, I got it! I got the job! Oh, my God! I can't believe it. Can you believe it? Durkin and Chestnut offered me a position in their firm. I'm going to be designing for the best firm in Tampa!" she squeals into my ear.

I sit up in bed, finally excited about something after the last twenty-four hours of regret and recriminations I've beat myself up with over running away from Cade like some scared rabbit. "That is so great! I knew you'd get it. They'd be crazy not to hire you with your experience. Ten to one they decided after your work on the Tamsin project."

She sighs into the phone at my mention of her favorite achievement since she started designing homes. "I loved working on that house. It will forever be the best time I ever had. Tamsin."

"The best until now."

"True. So we have to celebrate. Sabrina made reservations for us tomorrow night, so get out your best dress, girl, because we are celebrating."

"Okay. Sounds good!"

That part came out forced because while I love Meadow, her sister Sabrina can grate on my last nerve sometimes. She's like every Barbie doll, supermodel, and overachiever all rolled into one when she gets going after a few drinks.

Too perky, too perfect, and too much.

"She's going to send me all the particulars, so I'll text them to you when she gets them to me. Oh, Hailey, I'm so excited. The best design firm in the city wants me. I can't get over it. I keep pinching myself to see if it's really real."

"It's really real," I say with a chuckle at how adorable she is. "You deserve this. Twenty-five and on your way to the top. Will you remember us little people when you get there?" I tease.

"Of course," she answers, giggling. "How could I forget my friends who've always been there for me?"

"Make sure you mention us in your speech when you win designer of the year."

"I will. I have to go now. I feel like all my clothes for work look like rags, so I'm going to splurge on some new skirts and tops. Maybe even a suit to replace the one I've had all this time since I started. I can't wait to see you tomorrow night. As soon as Sabrina texts me the details, I'll send them along. Do you want to grab a ride with us, or are you flying solo?"

The thought of being trapped in a car with Sabrina to and from the restaurant, in addition to sitting at the table with her for dinner makes that answer easy. "I'll drive my car. Just let me know when and where and I'll be there with bells on."

Meadow is so delirious with happiness she's forgotten how her sister and I get along. That's okay, though. It's her night, so we can behave for a few hours and celebrate her success.

At least I can. As for Sabrina, I can't say.

"Great! It's going to be so much fun!" she squeals.

"Congratulations, Meadow. You deserve this. I'll see you tomorrow night."

I lay back on my bed and try not to let my jealousy get the better of me. I love Meadow like I love my sisters. She's been like a member of my family since we were kids in elementary school. I'm happy for her.

Really.

Meadow deserves everything she's getting. She's worked her ass off to make a name for herself in the design business around town. She's talented and disciplined.

Then why is it that all I feel as I lie here staring up at my bedroom ceiling is jealousy?

ALL DAY, I WAIT FOR HER TEXT AS I TRY MY HAND AT making rose cupcakes for the restaurant. They turn out better than I expected, and no sooner do I put the pink, white, and peach colored cupcakes out in the case, I finally get word from Meadow where we're going and what time.

Be at CK at six. Can't wait to see you!

CK. That's the restaurant Cade's cousin said he worked at. I stare down at my phone and wonder if I should text her back for the address or if she'll realize she forgot to send it. A second later, another text from Meadow makes my phone vibrate in my hand, and I see she did remember.

Money must be no object for Sabrina tonight since CK is one of the best restaurants in town. Definitely not in my usual price range, but for Meadow, I'll swing it.

Catching a glimpse of myself in the glass window of the display case, I grimace. I might be able to afford CK for one dinner, but with the way I look, I'll stick out like a sore thumb at a place like that.

Unfortunately, I don't have enough time to go shopping for a new outfit, so I'll just have to muddle through with that dress I bought last summer before everything happened. I close my eyes and try to push away the negative thoughts that immediately pop up in my mind.

So things went horribly wrong and your boyfriend cheated on you. It happens. At least you'll get to wear that dress you were supposed to wear to the rehearsal party.

I repeat those words over and over for a few moments, just like Dr. Thorpe always says to, and for the first time ever, it actually works. I take a deep breath in and let it out slowly—also a trick she swears by—and open my eyes to see my reflection staring back at me.

Still not great, but with some makeup and my trusty hair straightener, I'll look good enough for Meadow's celebration dinner. It doesn't really matter what I look like anyway. With her sister there looking like Miss Florida, who's going to notice?

"Is this place not the most gorgeous place you've ever seen?" Sabrina gushes as Meadow and I scan the menu.

Normally, her exaggerating gets on my nerves, but tonight she isn't overstating how incredible CK is. Dimly lit by lights in the ceiling, sconces on the dark colored walls, and lamps on end tables scattered around the restaurant, the bank of windows that takes up the entire wall facing out toward the water provides not only enough light but a breathtaking view.

Gorgeous is the least CK is.

"I feel like I've died and gone to heaven," Meadow whispers as she leans over toward me. "This menu has so many things that look so good. What are you thinking of getting?"

My eyes roam over the large parchment menu in my hands for a moment before I turn to face her. "I have no idea. Maybe the shrimp risotto?"

"You have to get the steak, Meadow," Sabrina says, interrupting us. "I've heard people say it's the best they've ever had. Something about the way they treat it or where they get it from. That's what I'm getting."

Meadow stifles a laugh and points at the steak section on the menu. "Steak with rosemary chimichurri? I can do rosemary, but I'm not always a chimichurri fan, Sabrina."

Her sister waves away her concern about the spiciness of the dish. "It'll be fine. Places like this never go full-tilt on the spice anyway."

I roll my eyes behind my menu, and as Meadow leans away to sit back in her seat, she says, "I'll think about it, but I'm really feeling salmon tonight. The only thing is I like it well-done. Do you think that will be a problem?"

Before I can say she's the guest of honor so she can have her salmon any way she likes, her sister leans in toward the center of the table shaking her head. "That's like blasphemy to chefs at a restaurant like this. You can't ask for that, Meadow. What's wrong with salmon like it's usually done?"

Meadow get a sheepish look and shrugs. "The texture is too soft. It makes eating it almost impossible."

"Then you have to get the steak. That's it. Steak it is."

We've been here fifteen minutes, and already I want to stick a fork through Sabrina's forehead. I promised I wouldn't say anything to make anyone uncomfortable tonight, but before I can stop myself, I mumble, "Why don't we let the woman who just scored the job of her dreams choose what she's going to eat and how she's going to eat it?"

Despite the fact that every table around us is filled with other people, I swear I can hear a pin drop when those words come out of my mouth. Meadow pulls her menu so close to her face that she can't possibly even see the words to read them, and I glare across the table at Sabrina with a death stare since I've already gone back on my promise to not get into it with her.

The entire scene feels like someone's put the world on slow-motion speed. Nobody seems to be moving around us, and all I can hear is the sound of my heartbeat pounding in my ears.

Sabrina glares back at me from across the table, her perfectly made up eyes with her fake lashes ever so slightly narrowed to let me know she didn't appreciate my little comment. Well, too bad.

"Meadow, you do what you want. Tonight is your night, so you don't have to listen to anyone."

Typical Sabrina. She gets bossy and then makes it

seem like everyone else is pressuring people to do things.

Lost in my disgust with how easy it is to predict Meadow's sister would act like this, I don't see the man approaching our table until he's right next to my elbow. I look up and see it's none other than Cade's cousin himself.

He smiles, showing off perfectly white teeth and lighting up his face so even his dark brown eyes seem to sparkle. I hadn't noticed how stunning he was that day, but now as he's standing over me looking down like he's happy to see me, I'm taken aback by how he looks, even in his chef uniform.

Oh, my God! I can't remember his name! What was it? Damnit, I can only remember Cade's name. He's going to think I'm so rude. He said such wonderful things about my cookies, and I can't even remember his name.

"Hailey, isn't it? The woman who makes the incredible desserts at Comfort Food?"

I give him a smile I hope hides the terror racing through me as I try to recall what his name was. Cade and... Oh, God. How could I have forgotten?

Finally, after a pregnant pause that surely must be making him wonder if I'm suddenly a mute, I say, "Hi! Yes, that's me. Thank you so much for remembering..."

His smile grows broader, and he finishes my sentence, mercifully. "Alex. It's great to see you again, Hailey. I don't remember if I mentioned where I worked, but I happened to look out and saw you sitting here, so I thought it would be only right that I came out to say hello to return the professional courtesy."

I smile and open my mouth to introduce everyone at the table to Alex, but Sabrina chimes in with, "Professional courtesy? Did you get a promotion, Hailey? I thought you made desserts at your parents' restaurant."

Every cell in my body screams for me to lash out at her for that little swipe at what I do, but I don't get the chance to even give her a nasty look before Alex says, "What Hailey does at her job is very much the same as what I do. If you can't see that, you need to look again at what she creates. She and I are equals when it comes to our professions."

Meadow squeezes my arm under the table, and I turn my head to see her gazing up at Alex like he's a fantasy come true. I can practically read her mind.

Gorgeous, great job, and so considerate.

Trying to beat Sabrina to the punch before she opens her mouth again, I quickly thank him and add, "Alex, this is my friend Meadow. Her sister Sabrina and I are here celebrating Meadow landing a job with the design firm of Durkin and Chestnut."

He graciously congratulates her and reaches out to shake her hand. I think Meadow might pass out she's smiling so much.

"Interior design? I should definitely call you because my place could use some real help. I'm ashamed to say it looks the same as it did the day I moved in, and that's not saying much. It's a combination of just graduated with bachelor, and it's not good."

Meadow presses her knee so hard against mine I'm afraid she's going to push me off my chair. She quickly rifles through her purse and hands him her business card. "I don't have any new ones made up yet since I just got the job, but this one has my number on it. Give me a call. I'd be happy to see what we could do to get that place of yours in much better shape."

"Will do," he says with a smile, and I notice he can't take his eyes off her.

"Well, I better get back to the kitchen or they're going to think I abandoned ship. Enjoy your meals ladies, and it was wonderful meeting you. Hailey, don't be surprised if Cade and I come back to Comfort Food to try more of your creations. I look forward to seeing what you make next time."

Alex gives us all one more smile and walks away. Sabrina lets out a disgruntled huff that I can't figure out, but Meadow and I let out a collective sigh before turning to look at one another.

"Okay, who is Cade and why didn't you tell me you met my future husband?" she asks with a giggle.

"Cade is his cousin. Yeah, I think that's it. He actually looks a lot like Alex. Maybe a few less tattoos. Or maybe more. I'm not sure. I only saw them together that one time. They stopped into the restaurant last week when I made chocolate lace cookies. I think that was Thursday."

Meadow scrunches her face up at me. "Stop getting lost in the minutiae. Tell me everything about them. Who are they? Why haven't I ever seen them before in my life? This city isn't that big."

"I don't know much more than you do. His name is Alex, and his cousin's name is Cade. He drives a red Jag. I do know that."

Her dark eyes get wide like saucers. "That man, the man who's the star of every fantasy of mine, drives a red Jag? I think I'm in love."

Shaking my head, I explain, "No, I don't know what he drives. Cade drives the Jag. Sorry."

Meadow lets out a sigh. "It's okay. I can live with Greek god who has a great job and is sweet and sexy no matter what he drives."

CHAPTER NINE

ade

ON MY WAY OUT THE DOOR TO DRIVE OVER TO THE club and do my time behind the bar for my father, my phone vibrates in my pocket. I consider not answering since it's probably just boss man wondering why I'm not in the building yet.

As if I need to be positioned behind the goddamned bar at six o'clock at night. Did he fire every other bartender he has in anticipation of having me work day and night there?

When I lift the phone out of my pocket, I see it's Alex calling and quickly answer. "Hey, I'm on my way to prison. What's up?"

"Prison? What are you talking about?" Alex asks, obviously confused by my attempt at humor.

"Club X. I'm doing my bartending gig tonight and

probably for the rest of fucking time. I'm guessing I have to wear all black and the white stripes come after a few months. Speaking of working, aren't you doing just that tonight?"

"Yes, and if you'd stop riffing about how much you hate your job, I'd be able to tell you what I called you about," he says, every word dripping with frustration.

I stop at my car and open the door to get in. "Nobody's stopping you, man. What's got you so upset tonight?"

"Not upset, and shut the hell up so I can tell you this. That Hailey girl is here with her two friends. They just ordered their meals, so get down here and coincidentally run into her."

"What is this? Eleventh grade and you found out where some girl's locker is so I can coincidentally run into her? Who the hell does that?" I ask as the thought of driving to this job makes me hate life.

"She looks really good, Cade. I just thought you might want to try your hand at getting to know her here. Maybe she won't run away this time."

Just what I need from my best friend—some ball busting about her running away from my last attempt. "Fuck you, man."

Alex laughs at my frustration. "Okay, don't then. I already made inroads with her friend, who is fucking hot, so you just stay at home alone or behind the bar dealing with drunk women and their slurring when they tell you how much they want to fuck you. Your choice. Either way, I have to get back to work."

The call ends, and I know I have a choice to make.

I can go to the club and do what I promised my father I would and hate every minute of it, or I can rush down to CK and hope to catch Hailey and maybe make some progress with her.

I press my foot on the gas and scream out of the parking lot of my condo toward the restaurant. No fucking way am I ready to give up a good time with a beautiful woman.

Not yet.

AFTER I SCHMOOZE THE MAÎTRE D' AND HAVE TO throw my family's name around to finally get in since I'm not dressed for CK, I catch a glimpse of Hailey sitting at a table in the middle of the restaurant. Good. I'm not too late, even though I swear every last soul in this damn city is out tonight and clogging up the streets.

I duck into the kitchen to find Alex before I try to chat Hailey up again, but I hear someone follow right behind me. Turning around, I see my uncle standing there smiling like something's amusing.

"What's up, Cassian?"

His eyebrows slowly raise up into his forehead. "I was going to ask you that very question. It's not every day you come waltzing into my kitchen."

I can't tell if he's angry or busting my ass, so I quickly give him a smile to smooth over whatever feathers I've possibly ruffled. "Just here to talk to Alex for a minute. I'll be out of here in no time."

Cassian nods, but I still don't know if he's pissed.

"I thought maybe you'd decided to come work for us after all these years. Your father told me you're going to be starting a new job soon, so I wondered if maybe I missed something and Kane hired you."

Okay. He's busting my balls.

"No, thanks. It's bad enough I have to go bartend at the club so I don't starve. At least I know how to pour drinks. Cooking food I have no idea how to do."

"Okay. Alex is over there," Cassian says, pointing toward his younger son.

I flash him another smile, and when he walks out of the kitchen, I hurry over to the kitchen doors to see if I can get another glimpse of Hailey. A second later, two servers nearly bash me in the head on their way in.

Jesus, is this a racetrack? I'm trying to see out this damn window, people.

"Cade, why are you getting in my staff's way?" Cassian says from behind me. "I thought you were here to see Alex, who is in the room you're in."

I turn around to answer him and another server comes bounding through the door, nearly knocking me over. I quickly step out of the way and over toward my uncle, who's giving me a look that says he's about to throw me out of this kitchen in about two seconds.

"Alex is the person I'm here to see. I just wanted to look out at the dining room. That's all."

Truly the dumbest thing I've ever said, and considering my past, that's pretty bad.

This time, Cassian gives me that single raised eyebrow look that says he's not buying a word of this bullshit. I don't blame him. I wouldn't buy it either. It wasn't my best attempt at concealing what I'm really doing.

"What's going on? You never come here, Cade, and now you're standing in my kitchen, blocking my servers' way, and staring out the window at my dining room."

No point in trying to lie anymore. It seems that I'm incapable of conjuring up a good enough answer, so I admit the truth. "Alex called me to let me know someone I've been interested in is here having dinner tonight. I was hoping to get a look at her before I go out there."

For a few seconds, Cassian doesn't seem to know what to do with that answer. It's the truth, but he probably doesn't believe it. Again, I don't blame him.

Then he finally smiles and says, "Is this how you usually meet women? You definitely take after your father if it is."

Just what I need—another reminder I'm like my father, or I'm supposed to be.

As Alex joins us in the corner of the kitchen out of the way of the staff, I answer my uncle's question. "No, it isn't how I usually meet women, thank you."

"Why are you still in here?" Alex asks before turning to his father. "The girl he likes is here tonight. I told him he should come down and talk to her. I don't think she'll run away here."

Of course, my uncle seizes on that wonderful tidbit of information and throws his head back in laughter. "Run away? Oh, I have to see this. Just don't make my restaurant look like some kind of crime scene she needs to flee from, Cade."

Hanging my head, I mumble, "I fucking hate this family sometimes. I really do."

"Awww, Cade. We're just teasing you," Alex says, not helping.

"Like father, like son with you two?" I ask, truly believing it was a mistake to come down here tonight. "This whole thing is stupid. She liked you better than she liked me."

"I already went out there and talked to her. Trust me. She isn't into me, and I already told you she isn't my type. Her friend, on the other hand, I'm all in on. Stop talking to us and go out there."

"Fine. I'll do it just to shut you two up. I swear this family sucks," I say as I walk out the kitchen doors into the dining room.

I look over at her table and see it empty. Fuck! All that talking to those two made me miss her.

Well, I'm not ready to give up just yet. I've already blown off my job for this attempt to talk to Hailey, so I might as well see it through. Hurrying around guests and tables, I run outside to find her walking to her car.

"Hey! What's new?" I call out as I do my best casual fast walk toward her.

"Are you stalking me or something?"

Not exactly the response I was hoping for. In fact, she's even chillier than the last time.

"What? No."

"Then why are you in this parking lot when I

know you weren't in the restaurant. You have no business being here."

Definitely not a good start to this attempt to get to know her. I try to be cool, but I have to explain I'm not some crazy stalker dude creeping up on her in a parking lot at night.

"I was in the restaurant and I have every reason to be here since my family owns this place. Well, not my immediate family but my uncles. My cousin Alex is a chef here."

She levels her gaze on me and hums as if she doesn't like what she's hearing. "I know. He came over to our table and was very gracious."

Great. Alex is gracious, and I'm a stalker who she might mace at any moment. I'm not thinking I could chalk that up to an improvement on our last meeting.

When she doesn't say anything more, I take a step toward her and ask, "So did you enjoy your meal? My uncles run a great place here."

"I have to go."

Not good. She doesn't even want to make small talk. Things are going from bad to worse. Well, not worse since she hasn't maced me yet.

"Would you like to go for a drink?"

She looks surprised at the question and doesn't answer for a long moment, so I hold out hope things are improving. Then with just a few words, she dashes my hopes.

"No. I have to go."

"Are you meeting your boyfriend now?"

"No," she says, shaking her head.

This is my in. I just have to finesse this right so she doesn't run away again. Or drive away, as the case may be this time.

"Then why not go for a drink with me? We can get to know one another. It could be fun."

Again, she shakes her head. "I don't really drink."

"Then let's go for a walk. You walk, don't you?"

That makes her smile, and I can't help but notice how beautiful she is when she smiles. It's like someone has lit her up from the inside.

"Of course I walk. Why are you so interested in me, Cade?"

A woman who gets right to the chase. I can appreciate that. No beating around the bush is the way she wants it, so that's what I'll do.

"Because you're beautiful and I liked that you were watching out that window in that kitchen door at your parent's restaurant the other day. After tonight, I know how dangerous that actually is and I appreciate it even more."

She narrows her eyes like she doesn't understand what I'm talking about, but that doesn't matter. I just need to get her to say yes to the walk.

One yes and we can see what happens next.

"So you walk. I do too, so let's do it together. We're right here at the Riverwalk, so why not?"

"Because you might be a serial killer," she says with a tiny smile.

"I'm not, but if you want, we can go back into the restaurant and my uncle and cousin can vouch for me. You might get trapped listening to stories about when

I was a kid, though, and to be honest, I'd rather not have that humiliation heaped on me tonight. I'm willing to go back in so you can hear I'm definitely not a serial killer, though. You decide."

Hailey rolls her eyes. "Don't try to make me laugh. I'm trying to be serious here."

"So am I. My uncle can't stop himself sometimes, and he loves to tell the story about when Alex and I were around seven and found his razor and shaved off our eyebrows. Or the one about when Alex's brother Cash heard about what happens when you stick someone's hand in warm water while they're sleeping. He got both of us that night."

The admission of two humiliating experiences from my childhood makes her giggle, and I watch her icy façade melt right in front of me. She really is so beautiful. I don't know why she pushes people away, or maybe it's just me she likes to push away, but I want to see more of this person standing here with me now.

"What happens when you put someone's hand in warm water while they're sleeping?" she shyly asks.

Good. I've got her curious.

"I'll tell you on our walk."

CHAPTER TEN

$\mathcal{H}$ailey

A MINUTE INTO OUR WALK AND I'M ALREADY regretting agreeing to this. Cade is charming and sexy, but there are very few people on the path with us. I assumed there would be a lot of people like always, but then I always come here during the day, not at eight o'clock at night.

"So does walking make you get quiet? I thought we were doing so well back there, but now you're back to not talking to me," he says in a sweet voice that should calm me.

It doesn't.

"I'm just hoping you're not an ax murderer."

He laughs, which only makes him more charming or more possibly a real ax murderer. "I've been accused of many things, but I think this is the first time anyone's ever wondered if I was an ax murderer. Personally, I don't see me as an ax guy. I'm more of a gun guy or even a knife guy."

I look at him and see him smiling. "That's not making me feel any better."

"Well, how about I tell you what happens with the warm water trick and then you'll know I'm not an ax murderer?"

That sounds like a non sequitur if I've ever heard one.

"How is that going to convince me you're not a serial killer or ax murderer? You're dressed in all black, so maybe I just got your crime wrong. Are you a burglar?" I ask, knowing I shouldn't be so worried.

People go for walks down here all the time. Maybe not tonight, but I'm sure they do other nights.

My questioning makes him chuckle. "Fair enough. Well, to prove I'm not an ax murderer, the fact that I can't fit an ax anywhere on me is all the proof I have."

He opens his arms to his sides and turns around for me, I guess so I can inspect him for that hidden ax. As much as I should be looking for some weapon stashed away somewhere, it's hard to concentrate on anything other than how great his body is.

Probably spends hours at the gym every day. Yep. That's what's wrong with him. He's an egotistical, self-involved guy whose sole focus is on his body.

With a smile that's entirely too sexy illuminated by the pathway lamp overhead, he says, "See? No ax. As for the black pants and black shirt, I was going to do a shift at my club, but I decided at the last minute to come down to CK because I heard you were there."

His explanation makes me more curious about him. "You have a club? What kind? Like a nightclub or a smaller bar?"

"First, I have to fulfill my promise to tell you about that gag Cash pulled on us that night. When you put someone's hand in warm water, they have to go to the bathroom. Like right then and there. So he did it to Alex first and then me since we were sleeping downstairs at Alex's house after playing video games for hours. Two ten year olds in sleeping bags full of piss."

He looks entirely too charming telling me what sounds like a horrible experience that at first I don't know how to react. I want to laugh since it's funny, but I don't want to be rude.

"Feel free to laugh. You should. Looking back, it was hysterical. My cousin Cash thought so that night when we both woke up drenched with him standing over us laughing until his sides hurt. My aunt and uncle didn't think it was so funny, though, and we got the last laugh watching him wash our smelly, wet clothes and the sleeping bags. And that's your introduction to the March family. Sorry to say this is a pretty common kind of story with us since there are five male cousins and only two females."

I finally let myself giggle at his description of that night, amused at how self-effacing he can be. "Are you and Alex around the same age? You said you were both ten, but you can't be born on the same day to brothers, can you? What are the odds of that?"

Cade shakes his head. "No. I'm three months older. Alex just seems older than me because he's more serious. Always has been. You should have seen him that night with his brother. I thought he was going to kill Cash he was so mad. Not that I wasn't mad, but Alex looked like he was going to rip him apart limb from limb."

As we walk, I try to imagine the man who was so nice and who came to my rescue when Sabrina hurled that not-so-veiled insult at me at the table that angry. "You know, I can't see him being like that. He was so sweet when he came over to introduce himself to my friend and her sister tonight. He didn't have to come out at all since we'd only met that once last week, and then he was kind enough to say he and I were peers professionally, which definitely isn't true."

"Alex meant that. He thinks you are colleagues," Cade says, but I sense in his voice he doesn't believe it either.

That's okay. I know my level when it comes to what I do. And everything else, for that matter.

"Well, that's very nice of him, but I think he was just being chivalrous after my friend Meadow's sister made a dig about my dessert making compared to his being a chef. She's not my biggest fan."

"Screw her. She doesn't know what she's talking about. I trust Alex on this."

For a moment, I don't know what to say. Cade seems uncomfortable after that brief outburst too and puts his hand on my arm to stop me from walking. Facing me, he lowers his head like he's embarrassed.

"Sorry about that. She's your friend's sister, so saying that wasn't cool."

God, he's cute. I imagine this man could talk the birds out of the trees, and the ones who didn't want to leave, all he'd have to do is give them one of his sad looks with those dark brown eyes of his and they'd willingly do as he asked.

"You don't have to be sorry. I don't like Sabrina much at all. The feeling's mutual too. She doesn't think highly about any part of me, but I don't usually say much to her in my defense when she takes her swipes at my job or how I look because I would never want to hurt Meadow. So no need to be sorry. I appreciated how Alex set her straight in his very professional way, and I appreciate what you said. Truth be told, I silently thought the same thing when she made fun of my dessert making tonight."

Cade's face brightens at hearing I'm not offended by his attack on Sabrina. "Okay, then back to screw her then."

We begin walking again, and thankfully, more people start to fill the pathway around us. Not that I feel like he's an ax murderer. I don't know if I ever felt that way, but no matter how good looking he is or how nice it felt to hear him come to my defense about what I do, I don't really know much about Cade. Better to be safe than sorry with an almost perfect stranger.

Breaking the silence, he says, "You know, you shouldn't think what you do is any less than any other chef. I admit I didn't understand what you do at first, but Alex set me straight. He's serious about food, and he says you're an artist. That's pretty impressive considering what your canvas is."

Excited to tell someone about the rose cupcakes I made today, I begin to explain what they looked like and how I sculpted the frosting to look like real flower petals. Halfway through my description, though, I stop myself.

"God, you probably don't want to hear about peach colored roses being my inspiration for these silly cupcakes," I say quietly, embarrassed that I let myself get so wrapped up in telling him about those stupid petals.

"No way," he says with a smile. "I loved listening to you talk about them. I was trying to imagine them the whole time you were describing them, but I'm not really creative, so I'm probably thinking all the wrong things. I don't honestly even know what a peach rose looks like. Is that a color or how they smell? You probably think that's pretty stupid, huh?"

"The peach is the color. I took a picture with my phone. Would you like to see it?"

"Absolutely!"

I reach into my purse and grab my phone, happy I changed my wallpaper the other day from that hot guy Meadow and I saw in that movie last month to a sunset scene. A few taps on the screen and the image of my cupcake creations from this afternoon comes up.

Turning my phone so Cade can see, I point at the frosting petals. "That's the peach rose cupcakes. I saw them online a couple days ago and wanted to try my hand at making them. I love how they turned out, and from the way customers at the restaurant grabbed them up, I think they were a hit."

Cade stares at my phone for a long moment and then looks up at me and gives me a smile. "You really are talented, Hailey. I couldn't do that if I had someone standing beside me giving me step-by-step directions, much less from only seeing a picture online. I bet they tasted incredible too, just like that cookie I had the other day."

I sheepishly admit the truth of how many I sampled before putting the rest out for customers. "Although I shouldn't have, I ate two of them, and although I'm completely biased, they were delicious. I made them as vanilla cupcakes this time and used a special ingredient. Sour cream. People sometimes get turned off when they hear that's part of my vanilla cupcakes, but it makes them taste so good! I'm thinking next time I want to try to make different flavors for each rose color, so peach cupcakes for the peach roses and vanilla for the white ones."

God, I meant to just say I ate two damn cupcakes and there I go again giving him every last tedious detail on cupcakes. Dr. Thorpe is right. Without practice around people my age, I've started to forget how to behave. I'm turning into a middle-aged woman before I reach twenty-five!

Looking away, I try to hide my embarrassment. "I'm sorry. This must be so boring for you walking around and talking about cupcakes."

"Not at all. I'm enjoying this a lot. You're passionate about what you do. There's nothing wrong with that," Cade says.

When I don't look over at him because I just feel so awkward still, he takes my hand in his and stops me from walking. Surprised and unsure what to say or do, I don't have a choice but to face him. I haven't been this close with a man since Malcolm, and my brain seems to shut off as I look at Cade now.

"Don't be ashamed for who you are. I'm having a great time listening to you talk about all of it—the cupcakes, the ingredients, even the color peach. Maybe it's because I've spent years listening to my best friend talk about food like it's something to be worshipped. I don't know. But if you're worried you're boring me, let me tell you, you're not."

"Maybe you could tell me something about you. I feel like I've been monopolizing the whole conversation, so you tell me about who you are for a while."

With a nod and one of his sexy smiles, he agrees to talk about himself, which will keep me from blabbering on about cupcakes and clue me into who Cade March really is. I know he's good-looking and very tolerant of my food obsession, but is there more to him?

As we begin down the pathway again, he keeps his gentle hold on my hand. At first, I wonder if I should pull away, but I push away that instinct that comes from fear.

"What do you want to know? I went to school up

north and graduated with a degree in business. It's the last thing I want to do in life, though, so I haven't used it much since I came back to town."

"But you own a club, so that must be useful for you to know all you learned in college," I say, instantly wishing I could brag about going to school without having to explain what happened.

His hand tightens around mine slightly for a moment before he eases his hold. "I guess, but real life is never the same as what you learn in school. I went to school because I had to. I graduated because I had to. I work because I have to."

Turning to look over at me, he smiles. "See, that's why listening to you talk about what you do is so interesting. You want to do that. You love what you do, and it shows when you talk about it. I don't love what I do, and I know how I sound when I talk about it."

I want to hear more about his club, but since he clearly doesn't enjoy his work like I do, I quickly change the subject. "Well, what do you do when you're not working?"

With a chuckle, he answers, "I've just now decided I'm the most boring person in the world. I don't do much when I'm not working. Alex and I hang out on his days off, and sometimes our other cousins join us and we go jet skiing. Alex's father has a boat, so we go fishing too."

He looks at me and winces. "I think we should go back to talking about cupcakes or you're going to decide you never want to see me again because I have no life."

I give him a sympathetic smile and try to think he's a boring guy who does nothing. I can't, though. He's not boring at all, and if I'm not careful, I'm going to find myself letting him past all those walls I've so carefully constructed this past year.

CHAPTER ELEVEN

ade

THE TIME I SPEND WALKING ALONG THAT PATH WITH Hailey and talking like we've known each other forever is the best hour of my day. I knew my instincts weren't wrong about her, even if she ran away from me the other day.

She's every bit as incredible as I'd built her up to be in my mind. Passionate and committed to her work, she's also sweet and sexy and not that shy once she gets talking.

All I had to do was make the effort and it paid off. Now I want to see how far we can take this thing between us.

We get back to her car and I sense she's nervous because she's gone quiet on me again. She lowers her head, fixing her gaze on the ground while I talk about anything that pops into my mind so our time together doesn't have to end. I'd much rather stand here talking gibberish than go to the club to serve drunks for the rest of the night.

"So what do you think about doing this again? How does tomorrow night sound?" I ask as I take a step closer to her.

But she doesn't look up at me when she answers, "Tomorrow night? I don't know."

"You had fun, didn't you? You got to hear about me pissing the bed and how my family is one step away from insane ninety percent of the time. And I got to find out about what makes peach roses peach, which I guess I should have known by this point in my life, but to be honest, I don't think most guys know exactly what the color peach is. We lump that in with salmon and colors like mauve, which I have no idea what it looks like but I'm guessing it's like peach."

Hailey finally lifts her head and looks at me, smiling at my color ignorance. "Mauve is not like peach," she says with an adorable giggle. "As for salmon, I guess I can see why you might get that confused with peach."

I take another step toward her, shrinking the space between us to only a couple inches. She really is so beautiful right now looking up at me with those crystal blue eyes that seem to sparkle under the streetlight above where her car is parked.

"Now I know the surefire way to get you to talk is to show you how stupid I am about something. Good to know."

She tilts her head like she isn't sure if I'm being serious or not and she wants to decide before saying anything else. "I don't think you're stupid about colors. You're just a guy. Guys think of things in basic colors. Black, white, blue, red, green, yellow and maybe orange is pretty much all men consider when it comes to colors, so you're no different than anyone else and definitely not more stupid."

The way she tries to make me feel better about being so utterly ignorant about something she understands so well charms me. I'm not even sure she realizes how sexy it is that she's sweet like that.

Still, I like the banter that's part of the chase with any woman, so I put on my fake sad face and tease her about saying I'm no different than anyone else. "So I'm just like every other guy you've ever met? Ouch. That hurts a guy's ego, and we're practically all ego, you know."

Instinctively, she waves her hands in front of her, brushing up against my chest since I'm so close now. "I didn't mean it that way. No, I don't think you're like everyone else. I don't. Really."

Leaning down, I stop her explanation with a kiss I've been dying to sneak since she started talking about those delicious sounding cupcakes nearly an hour ago. Her lips are soft, and although I've been nearly hard for the past few minutes, just the touch of her mouth on mine makes my cock stiffen so it's pressing against the front of my pants.

She returns my kiss with a soft kiss of her own and lets her palms graze my ribs as with each second that ticks by she relaxes more and more. I lift my hand to caress her cheek, but that startles her and she quickly pulls away.

"I should go. It's getting late," she says, looking down at the ground again.

"Tomorrow night then."

My making a date for us without her agreeing makes her lift her head, but I don't see anger in her eyes when she looks at me. If anything, I see fear. Why? She can't still think I'm an ax murderer, can she?

"I don't know if I can, Cade," she says in a shaky voice.

"Why? You had fun. I know you did. You smiled. You laughed. You talked about things that make you happy. Sounds like the kind of time you'd tell people about and say I'm a fantastic guy. I know I'd tell people I had a great time tonight and you're definitely a fantastic woman. So what's the problem?"

Her eyebrows draw in and she frowns for the first time since she accused me of stalking her here in the parking lot tonight. I instantly hate that frown on her. I hate that I had some part in putting it there even more.

"I'm not really good at things like this," she says shyly.

"Talking and walking? Don't sell yourself short. I think you've mastered those quite well," I say with a smile.

My attempt at a joke doesn't get me a smile in return, but at least her frown eases a little. "I have, yes, but everything that comes after that with someone I'm not good at."

"I can tell you you're great at kissing, so put that in the mastered column with walking and talking."

She lets out a heavy sigh and finally says what I suspect has been on her mind since the day we met. "Why are you interested in me? I don't drive an expensive car like you do. I work in a little restaurant that's nothing like the one your family owns and I doubt it's as impressive as your club. I'm not the type of girl who a guy with a red Jag wants, so why do you keep coming around?"

Taking her hand, I bring it to my mouth to press a kiss against her knuckles. "I like you because you're you. I don't know why I was interested in you that day I saw you looking out the kitchen window at me. I just was from that day. I don't care what kind of place you work in. I think you're interesting and fun, and you're talented at what you do. You're also beautiful, and why wouldn't a guy with a red Jag want you?"

"Because I don't have legs that go on forever. Just regular legs on my five foot five body. My hair isn't gorgeous and most of the time it stays up in a ponytail. Look at the way I'm dressed. Red Jag women wear little dresses that show off the goods. I'm in a navy blue sundress that's nothing special. I just wonder if someone like me belongs talking to someone like you," she says before pressing her lips together, as if she needs to stop herself from saying anything more.

Hailey isn't wrong. I've spent most of my life chasing after women who look like they should be in a red Jag. I've had a lot of them too, but they want me for what I have, especially how much money I have. The fact that this is the first time she's even mentioned my car and still hasn't asked me to take her for a ride tells me what I have doesn't matter to her.

Maybe that's why I like her. Because she doesn't want anything anyone else has from me before.

"I like the way you look and the way you dress. To be honest, I don't care what you do with your hair or what you wear. From the first moment I saw you, I wanted to know more about you. Then I found out you were just like Alex, except way prettier."

Hailey smiles at my joke, so I continue. "I figure if he and I can get along famously for all these years as best friends, maybe you and I can be together and have a good time. You're both into your work in the same field, and while I don't do much with food other than stuff it into my mouth, I like being around someone who cares that much about what they create that they could talk about it for half a mile."

"You have a way of putting things that makes me want to say yes to you. Are you like this with everyone?"

I think about the talk with my father earlier and can't stop myself from grimacing. He's going to bust a blood vessel when I finally get to the club tonight, and I'd be willing to bet all my trust fund that he won't want to say yes to anything I say to him.

"Sadly, no. My charm and persuasive abilities do not work on everyone. I like that they work on you, though. Tomorrow night we can go for another walk again or do anything you want. You name it and we'll do it."

"Okay. I'll text you since I have your number," she says, giving away that she kept my note.

If she'd thrown it away, I might have to do a lot more persuading, but knowing she decided to keep it, even after running away from me that day, tells me things might be going better than I had thought.

"Text or call me anytime. Until tomorrow night, thanks, Hailey."

Confusion fills her expression. "For what? All we did was walk and talk a little while."

"For not thinking I'm like everyone else."

I can't tell if her eyes get wide out of fear that she might be wrong and I am like every other guy or fear that's she right. As long as I have another chance to get to know her even more, I'll show her just what I am.

And how much I want her.

"Wakey, wakey," I hear a voice say above me. "Are you going to spend all day in bed?" it taunts.

Am I dreaming, and if I am, why am I dreaming some asshole is waking me up? I need to reconsider what I eat right before I go to bed if this is the quality of dreams I'm having.

Slowly, I open my eyes to see Alex standing at the side of my bed. Covering my eyes with my arm, I groan. "Go away."

"We're supposed to go jet skiing today, remember? Time's wasting. I've got until four to have fun, so get up out of that damn bed and let's get going."

I lower my arm and see he's still here. His hazy figure doesn't move from where he stands. He's planning on forcing this issue. I don't even remember making plans to do anything today. What day is it?

"Give me ten minutes and come back then. Thanks," I say before rolling over and covering my head with the pillow.

He rips the pillow from my grip and tosses it across the bed out of my reach. "Nope. Time to get up, sleeping beauty."

With a sigh, I try to not let all the aggression building up inside me out on my best friend, but it's hard. Very fucking hard.

"You sound like my father. Are you sure you're not his kid? Because you're both fucking slave drivers," I mumble into the bed.

"Come on, Cade. It's nearly noon, for Christ's sake. It's a beautiful day, although you'd never know since you keep this place like a fucking morgue. The sun's out, the water's waiting for us, so let's go."

I struggle to sit up, still half-asleep and exhausted from getting home after four. "You have no respect for the dead. None whatsoever."

"Did you work at Club X last night? Your father must kept you there until he locked the doors," Alex says with a chuckle.

Like any part of that reality is even slightly amusing.

"Fuck off and go jet skiing by yourself, dick."

From across the bed, he hurls a pillow at me, hitting me in the head and knocking me over. "Get up, man! And you haven't told me anything that happened with Hailey yet. Did you get anywhere with her?"

"Things went great. I have a date with her tonight. Why are you interrogating me first thing in the morning? Did you at least bring me something to wake up with? Coffee? Energy drink?"

"I'm not your butler, man. Get your own caffeine. So you got a date with her tonight? Good."

Setting my feet on the floor, I slowly stand from the bed as I gradually come alive. "Yeah, good. She's going to pick the place and the time. I'm letting her do all the work."

"Why?" Alex asks, like he's horrified at the suggestion that I'm not dictating every minute of our time together.

I scrub the last remnants of a wonderful, albeit short night's sleep from my face and pad across the room toward the bathroom. "Because I thought I might not give her any reason to fucking run away again. Sometimes you don't come in like a goddamned wrecking ball. Sometimes you use the velvet hammer to get what you want. I think I know why you're single, dude. These are simple concepts."

By the time I get out of the bathroom, I'm wide awake. Well, as wide awake as I can be without some serious infusion of caffeine.

"You know, some people actually call or text before

coming over to wake people up, dude," I say as I walk toward the kitchen. "Try it sometime."

"Sorry. I'm not used to you working, Cade. I just figured you'd be lounging around when I got here."

Alex sounds almost like he feels bad, so I give him a whatever shrug and grab a water from the refrigerator. Standing in the doorway, he watches me drink, but I have the sense he's got something on his mind.

"I feel like one of those animals in the zoo with you staring at me like that. 'The wild Cade, newly awake, saunters down to the watering hole, noticing in the distance a far too alert Alex keeping a watchful eye on him.' What's up?"

For a moment, he hesitates to answer my question, piquing my interest even more. I know Alex as well as I know myself, so the fact that I have no idea what may be on his mind makes me think I'm not as awake as I thought I was.

"Are you going to tell me, or am I supposed to read your mind? I mean, we've known each other practically since birth, but I don't think we've developed that skill yet."

"Are things going to be different with this one?" he asks in a tone so full of what sounds like judgment that I'm stunned for a second.

"Things? Like what things? Are you asking if I'm going to buy different clothes to go out with Hailey or if I'm planning on trying out some new sexual positions? Because it would be a no to the clothes but maybe to something freaky, assuming she's into that."

My smart ass answer doesn't satisfy him, if the scowl he gives me is any indication. I know what he's talking about. I just don't want to tackle that issue regarding Hailey yet. Things are going good between us so far. There's no reason to think they'll crash and burn.

Like they do with every woman I date.

"She's a nice girl, Cade. She's talented and sweet, and from what I saw last night, she's not a bitch, even when it calls for her to be one."

I take another swig of cold water and try to keep my cool, even though I'm quickly losing it. "I know she is. And she told me how you stood up for her when that friend's sister tried to say she isn't a chef like you. What's this about, Alex?"

It's been a long time since we had a knock-down, drag-out fight, but I have a feeling that might be happening instead of the jet skiing today by the way he's looking at me right now. His eyes narrowed, he looks pretty fucking judgmental, and I'm not feeling that.

"Say what's on your mind."

He doesn't need any more than that to tell me what he's thinking about me with Hailey. "Well, how about we go over your recent history with women, shall we? There was Cassie, who you couldn't get enough of but she found out you lied to her about who you were and she said adios. Before her was Emma. That crashed and burned pretty quickly, and why? You lied to her about who you were. How about before her? Amber, I think. And what happened there? Lied."

"Fuck off, Alex."

I push past him to go into the living room, but he follows me, continuing with his dissertation on my love life. "And the worst of it is you lie about bullshit stuff. Why lie about how you could afford the Jag? It's not like Cassie thought you were some Silicon Valley whiz kid who had come up with the replacement for Facebook, Cade. And Emma? With her, you lied about this condo and said you shared it with me, which was ridiculous."

"You're here often enough that it was only technically a stretch of the truth."

"And what was it with Amber? Well, that was a huge whopper. You lied about being single since you were still with Sarah. So I guess you can include her in with Amber's lie."

I point the water bottle at him, intent on at least defending myself on that point. "We were technically not together anymore. She had ignored my calls for three days. That said to me we were done. So you can't count either of those as lies. And in my defense, I didn't lie to Sarah and that ended, so I think your entire thesis about my lying leading to the end of all of my relationships is total bullshit."

"Yes, you did. You told her you were going to be managing your father's club, which we both know you never planned to do. So you did lie."

That very lie I told Hailey last night flashes through my mind, and I turn my head so I don't have to face Alex. As I said, we've known each other for nearly our entire lives, and while we can't read each other's minds, I doubt he'll miss the look I know is on my face as I remember telling her I manage the club.

"Dude, you lied to her already, didn't you? What's wrong with you? This sounds pathological."

I wave away his concern, pretending it's nothing. "I just told her I was doing something I'm not exactly doing. That's all. We barely know each other, so it's not a problem."

"You lied about managing Club X, didn't you? Why do you do that? It's not like you're some poor guy mooching off his parents and living in their basement. Look at this place. You own it. Like your car. And the jet skis. And everything else you have because of your trust fund. Most guys in your place brag about that kind of shit, and yet you insist on lying. Why?"

I spin around, not worried about what expression I have on my fucking face now. "Stop busting my balls. I don't have to let any woman know about my finances. Do you go around sharing your bank account balance with every woman you get into bed with?"

"That's not the point and you know it."

"If all you're going to do is lecture me, then leave me alone. You sound like my father."

The insult hits just like I wanted it to, and Alex shakes his head. "I sound like me. She's sweet, and you're already lying. This isn't even about you hurting her because, fuck, I barely know Hailey. This is about you sabotaging every relationship you have. You love the chase. You're notorious for it, and I have no problem with that. But you've got a problem, Cade. This lying isn't okay."

On my way back into my room, I yell back to him, "You know the way out. Don't slam the door when you leave."

A minute later, I'm back in bed and I hear my best friend close the front door when he walks out. Nice start to the day.

CHAPTER TWELVE

ailey

MY FATHER STOPS AT MY DOUGH TABLE AND RAPS his knuckles off the metal rack next to it. "You've got a visitor out front, honey."

I lift my head from the cupcake I've been frosting and look at him in shock. A visitor to see me? "Who?"

"One of the guys from the other day. I don't remember his name. They both look alike, so I'm not sure which one."

Quickly, I tear off my gloves and look at my reflection in the metal case next to me to see if I got any cupcake batter or frosting on my face or in my hair. I don't see any, but I want to make sure, so I turn toward my father.

"Do I look okay? Too much a mess?"

A slow smile lights up my father's face. "You look beautiful, like always, honey."

Pushing the hairs that have escaped my ponytail from my face, I roll my eyes. "You're not helpful, Dad. Okay, I'm going to go out there."

"Knock 'em dead, honey."

I throw him a look like I can't believe he said that and hurry out into the dining room before stopping dead just outside the doors. I'm still wearing my apron. Damn! I hurriedly pull it over my head and toss it onto the counter near the sink.

Now I look presentable enough to see Cade.

Looking around the restaurant, I don't see him, though. I don't see anyone who looks like a male in his mid-twenties. The only customers around are the usual old men who sit at the counter forever drinking cup after cup of coffee and a family in one of the booths near the windows.

"Hailey, hey," a male voice says behind me.

I turn around and see Alex, not Cade. Why is his cousin here? Oh, God. He's here to tell me Cade doesn't want to be bothered with me because I waited too long to text him. I was going to do it after I finished that batch of cupcakes.

"Hi, Alex. What are you doing here?" I ask, hating how rude that sounds considering how nice he was about what Sabrina said at dinner last night.

"I had some free time this afternoon since my plans fell through, so I thought I'd stop in and see what you're making today. I looked in the case but didn't see anything. Did they sell out already?"

"No. Well, yes, but I was just working on some more cupcakes. I can show you them if you like."

Alex gives me a warm smile and nods. "Great. I'd love to see them."

"Okay. Come back into the kitchen," I say as I turn to head back to my station. Then I realize he's probably used to the best chef's kitchen, which is definitely not what we have here, so I stop and spin around to face him.

"I should warn you this probably isn't what you're used to a kitchen looking like."

"It's not the kitchen that makes great food. It's the chef, so don't worry."

Forcing a tortured smile I know isn't reaching my eyes, I move toward the kitchen silently praying to God Hector cleaned up and my father hasn't made another mess back there. It's bad enough my area looks like a cake factory exploded around it.

My hands are shaking by the time we walk through the doors. The moment I step foot inside, I frantically scan the kitchen for anything horrible, but it looks okay.

Well, okay for what I'm used to. What Alex works in probably looks like a million bucks compared to here.

I listen for any gasp of horror coming from him as we make our way to my table, but I don't hear anything but the usual sounds of the kitchen. The afternoon cook, Sylvie, is humming some tune she said reminds her of when she was a girl back in Austin, the ice machine is making that ka-chonk-a-chonk noise that tells me someone needs to kick it again, and my father's radio way back in the corner plays some Beach Boys' song I recognize but can't for the life of me remember the title right now.

"My area is back here," I say, pointing to where I left the cupcakes I'd been working on in the corner nearest to the doors.

Before I can say anything else, Alex stops in front of my table and looks down at the last of the peach cupcakes I'd just started when my father said I had a guest. "That looks exactly like a rose, Hailey. It's uncanny. If I didn't know it was a cupcake beneath that frosting, I'd say you'd sculpted an actual flower. What flavor did you use for the cake?"

His compliment makes me beam with pride. "I decided to do a peach cupcake for this color icing. I'd offer you one, but our customers bought them all up this morning and I'm saving this one for something special. I have vanilla ones, though. Would you like one of them?"

With a smile that reminds me of his cousin, he nods eagerly. "I'd love to try one."

Reaching around, I grab a white rose cupcake and hand it to him. "It's just a cupcake, you know. Nothing terribly special. These are more of an artistic project for me. I saw a picture of some online and wanted to see if I could do it."

"Can we sit in a booth and talk for a few minutes?" he asks. "I won't take up too much of your time."

I hope he can't see how surprised I am that he wants to sit with me when I smile and start moving back out to the restaurant. "Sure. That would be great."

When we're settled in a booth in the corner away from everyone else in the dining room, Alex takes his first bite of the cupcake. "This is delicious. You have to put something special in these because they don't taste like ordinary vanilla cupcakes."

"I do. Sour cream. It makes them taste so good, doesn't it?"

"Mmmm...that's it. I thought maybe I tasted a hint of almond, but sour cream makes sense. This is fantastic, Hailey. I hope the next time you make the peach ones I'm around and can grab one before everyone else buys you out. I bet they're out of this world."

As much as I want to talk shop with him and explain how I use pieces of fresh peaches in the batter, I'm too curious about why he's here and why Cade isn't with him to let myself gush about my recipe ingredients. Maybe he came alone because Cade's busy, or is it that he's not interested in me or my cupcakes?

"So what would you like to talk about?" I ask quietly, bracing myself for his response being that he's here to be the one to break it to me that his cousin doesn't want to see me again after all.

He reaches across the table to grab a napkin from the dispenser and wipes his mouth. "So good. Well, let me get right to the point. I showed my father and uncle the picture of the chocolate lace cookie I had here last time and they want to know what they'd have to do to be able to get your desserts on a regular basis for CK. Our customers would love them. We'd be willing to pay you well, of course."

Relief washes over me as he makes his offer, every word making me smile even as I know I have to decline. "I wish I didn't have to say no, but I can't do it, Alex."

He frowns, but I don't think he's unhappy as much as disappointed. "Is this because you don't think your desserts are good enough? They are, Hailey. Trust me."

Hearing him say that makes me want to burst into tears I'm so happy, but he's wrong. While I may not be the most confident baker in the world, that's not the reason why I have to say no to him and his family.

"Thank you, but no that's not why. I just don't have the time or facilities to make more than I do for my parents here. I'm trying to help them bring in more business."

I look around the restaurant at the mostly empty tables and booths and sigh. "I thought if people had something to come in for, they'd come back again and again. So far, it hasn't turned out like that, but I'm still hoping. I have to keep making my desserts for them, so after that, I don't have enough time or the right equipment to say I'll be able to contract with you to make enough for CK. I'm sorry, Alex. Please tell your father and uncle I'm so flattered. Last night was my first time at your restaurant, and to think that a place like that would want to sell my desserts is almost too incredible to believe."

"I understand. What you're doing for your parents is a good thing, Hailey. Just keep us in mind if you ever get the chance to branch out, okay?" he asks with a smile that's like a cherry on top of this beautiful cake his visit's been.

"Absolutely."

When he doesn't continue the conversation, I can't stop myself from mentioning Cade for the first time. "You know, I saw your cousin last night after my friends and I left the restaurant. We're supposed to get together again tonight."

"I think I heard something about that," he says with a sparkle in his dark brown eyes.

"He told me about his club, so maybe he'll show me that tonight."

Something in Alex's expression changes so imperceptibly it's almost not visible, but I sense the difference in him immediately. "Maybe. I have to get going, but keep my offer in mind, okay?"

And with that, he stands from the table and gives me one last smile. "Take care, Hailey."

"Thank you, Alex."

As I watch him walk toward the front door, I can't help but wonder what made his mood change so suddenly. Was it the mention of Cade's club? Is there something he doesn't approve of in that, or is it that he doesn't think I'm the type of person who belongs at a place like that?

I press the piece of paper with Cade's phone number on it against the table, smoothing the wrinkles and creases from it being in my pocket all day. My hands tremble as I hold my phone, ready to text him. Am I ready for this? Dr. Thorpe says I am. Meadow thinks I'd be crazy if I didn't at least give myself a chance with Cade.

Then why do I feel like a nervous wreck when I even think about seeing him tonight?

My mind whirls with what could happen, what might go wrong, what it would be like to kiss him again. Pushing all that out of my head, I smooth the paper one final time and press the numbers into my phone before beginning my text.

Hi, this is Hailey. Hope you're having a great day. If you still want to get together tonight, I'm free.

I stare at the words, reading them over and over and wishing they sounded sexy or even fun, instead of such boring words. Of course I'm free. I'm always free. He probably knows that.

Maybe I should mention our kiss last night. But what am I going to say? Hey, thanks for kissing me? Your lips are soft? You have nice breath?

Definitely not. I'll just leave the text as it is. He's already met me. He must know by now I'm not exciting or sexy.

Or the type of woman who belongs in a red Jag.

I send it off, surprised that my anxiety doesn't abate but only gets worse. He might not reply. He might have decided after last night that he's not interested. I mean, if he was really into me, he could have come over with Alex this afternoon. Then again, maybe that's why Alex got so uncomfortable and left so quickly right after I mentioned Cade.

God, I wish I was a red Jag kind of woman.

While I mentally spiral out of control, my phone vibrates against the tabletop. I look down to see his response to my text and smile.

Meet me at CK at eight. See you then.

CHAPTER THIRTEEN

 ailey

ABSOLUTELY SURE I LOOK LIKE AN OVEREAGER teenage girl, I get to CK ten minutes early. I'd expected traffic to be heavier, but the drive took much less time than I thought it would. I could drive around, but then I might get stuck somewhere and be late.

It's fine. I can check my makeup in the rearview mirror since I have a few minutes.

I pull into a parking space and turn the car off before turning it back on. Looking down my body, I frown at my pink sundress. It looks so silly. I should have chosen something sexier.

That's a ridiculous idea. I don't own anything sexy. That's sort of the problem, isn't it?

"You're going to have to get out of the car for us to have any fun."

Spinning my head to look out my window, I see Cade standing outside smiling at me. "What? I didn't think you'd be here so early."

He looks incredible in jeans and a grey dress shirt. How does he do that? He's casual but sexy at the same time.

And I'm whatever the opposite of that is.

"Are you ready to go?" he asks before opening my car door.

"I guess," I say tentatively as I put up the window and turn off the engine. "Where are we going?"

"Are you hungry? We can get something to eat," he suggests when I step out of the car.

"Not really, but if you are, we can."

"I'm not, so cross eating off the list."

I want to ask if he would want to show me his club, but I keep that idea to myself. Something about the way Alex reacted earlier hints at that being an issue of some kind.

"We could go for a ride. Then you'd be able to definitely say you're a red Jag kind of girl. You already are, but that would make it official."

He slams my car door shut and guides me to his car on the other side of the parking lot. So now I become a red Jag girl. Not sure how that's going to look.

"So, other than sitting in a red Jag, what does a red Jag kind of girl have to do? I feel like I should have studied or something. Is there a handbook? Maybe that would be good for me to look at first," I say, hoping my jokes sound as funny as they do in my head.

But Cade isn't smiling. In fact, he looks like he's sizing me up like animals do with their prey. Oh, God. He is an ax murderer!

Just as we reach his car, he stops and leans in to kiss me. "You don't have to do anything but be you. Whatever that is, that's what a red Jag girl does as long as you're in the car. Easy, right?"

When his lips touch mine, I can't think of anything but how good he kisses. Gorgeous, has a hot car, and an incredible kisser. God, is there anything wrong with this guy?

If so, I don't want to know. Not right now, at least. Let whatever his flaws are come out later after I've enjoyed this night.

AN HOUR LATER, HE PULLS INTO A PARKING LOT AND points at the white building in front of us. "What do you think of doing something other than riding around for a while?"

"Is this where you live?"

"Yeah. I figured we could hang out for a while, but if you want to go somewhere, just tell me and we're there."

Again, I consider mentioning his club, but since it's only nine o'clock at night, it's highly unlikely the place is busy yet. I may not be a club kind of girl, but I do know things don't start happening until much later in the night.

"No, we can hang out. That's okay. This place looks nice. Do you live on your own?"

Cade turns the car off and nods. "Yeah. Sometimes I tell people I live with Alex, but you get the truth. It's just me."

I want to ask why he lies about a thing like that, but he jumps out of the car before I can and then a few seconds later, he's at my door opening it for me. Maybe he was kidding? Does he really tell other people that?

Instead, I ask what seems like a more obvious question at this moment as I crane my neck to look up at the enormous building looming in front of me. "What floor do you live on?"

Maybe that's why he's in such good shape. Walking up twenty flights of stairs each day would make anyone look good.

"One of the upper floors. Wait until you see the view from the balcony. It's what makes living here all worth it," he says like the beautiful surroundings, professional landscaping, and gorgeous building aren't enough.

"Oh. I bet you have a lot of very successful neighbors."

Cade shakes his head and grimaces. "Actually, I have a lot of old neighbors who complain and make up ridiculous rules at the HOA meetings. The last one I went to some lady raged on and on about someone's Christmas wreath being a choking hazard for like a half hour. I haven't been back since then."

I can't tell if he's serious, so as we walk into the main lobby, I look at him and smile. "Really?"

He nods but returns my smile. "I wish I was joking. This building wasn't like this when I bought the place. I figure I'm young enough to wait them out, though, so maybe in a few years it won't be bad. Or maybe I'll move. For now, the view from the balcony makes it all worth it."

I look around for a stairwell, but Cade guides me toward a bank of elevators that I silently thank God for. As the doors close, I watch him press the button for the fifteenth floor, and then the elevator starts moving up.

"This is a very smooth elevator," I say, suddenly nervous and needing to make small talk.

For a moment, Cade doesn't say anything, but then he laughs. "Yeah, I guess it is. I never noticed that. I think I'm usually so preoccupied about just getting to my place that I don't pay much attention at all to the ride."

He likely thinks I'm the most boring person in the world to pay attention to the smoothness of the elevator ride in his building. I couldn't argue with him if he did. So much for the ride in the Jag making me a red Jag girl. I bet the other women he brings to his home don't comment on the smooth elevator ride up.

I feel something against my pinky and look down to see him taking my hand in his. When I look up at him, he gives me one of his all-too-sexy smiles that make me feel like my insides are melting.

"You don't have to worry, Hailey. I'm not an ax

murderer, and this is just us going to hang out. Honest."

His touch calms me, but I still have to make a joke. "You know, I think only real ax murderers say they aren't ax murderers. Non-ax murderers don't say anything about not being one."

His smile broadens, and he leans down to kiss me, taking my breath away this time as the elevator stops at the fifteenth floor. "Point taken. Now if you see any wreaths, don't eat them, okay? I hear they're dangerous."

We walk down the hallway to his apartment as one thought fills my head. How is it possible this man is single?

God, I really hope he's not an ax murderer.

He opens his front door and says, "Welcome to my world. Excuse the mess. The maid hasn't been here this week."

No sooner do those words leave his mouth, Cade stops and turns around to face me wearing a look so earnest I'm not sure what he's going to say. "I don't have a maid. That was more of a joke than anything else."

"Oh, okay. I don't either, so it's not like I'm going to look down on you for having to straighten up your own mess."

"Good. Well, come in and relax. I'll get us something to drink. Alcohol or no?" he asks as he walks into another room.

"No alcohol, thanks."

I quickly scan the living room he's left me in. Open

to the dining room with an actual table and chairs set that doesn't look like it's ever been used as anything other than a place for Cade to drop his mail, this room contains a sectional that takes up most of the space. The walls are painted a tan color that doesn't clash with the black couch or the dark wood tables. It looks like a normal room a person would expect from a grown man.

Nothing in this room says he's a murderer or that he has a wife stashed away and this is his place where he cheats on her.

Cade hands me a glass of sparkling water and sits down next to me with a bottle of beer. "So this is my house. I'd give you a tour, but you're sitting in the highlight."

"I thought the best part was the balcony and the view," I tease and then take a drink of raspberry flavored water.

He takes the glass from me and sets it down onto the coffee table nearby, along with his beer. Grabbing me by the hand, he pulls me from the couch like a little boy eager to show someone what he's done.

"That's right. I forgot."

We walk past the dining room table filled with mail, and I quickly look to see if any say Mrs. March but I don't see any. Maybe he's just a man with good taste in apartments who seems too perfect. That can happen, right?

Sliding the glass doors open, he steps out onto a balcony that's much larger than I thought it would be and extends his arm like he's offering me the view for my own. "This right here is the highlight. Forget inside. This is it. What do you think? Gorgeous, huh? It makes having to live around crazy people terrified of wreaths all worth it."

I step forward and stop short, stunned by this view he has any time he walks out onto his balcony. Warm yellow and white lights around the bay cast shimmering reflections on the water, and the dark night sky with what seems like a million stars looks so close it's like you can touch it if you reach out.

"This is beautiful, Cade. You must love being able to look out whenever you want and see this."

He moves behind me and sets his chin on my shoulder. "I like how it makes you look."

My heart races at the feel of him pressed up against the back of me. "What do I look like?" I ask in a shaky voice.

Please don't let him be the kind of murderer who throws women off balconies.

"Your eyes got big and you looked out like you couldn't get enough of what you're seeing. I like that," he says in a low voice, his warm breath drifting over the shell of my right ear.

I want to say something but my mind is blank, except for loving how he feels pressed against me. Closing my eyes, I revel in the sensation, and when he slides his arms around my waist, I don't flinch.

And for the first time in a year, I don't fear someone holding me in their arms.

CHAPTER FOURTEEN

 Cade

HAILEY DOESN'T MOVE WHEN I GENTLY PULL HER TO me, and for a moment, I'm not sure what to think about that. By this time, most women are crawling up my body after seeing the view and me giving them all the signs.

Then again, she's not like anyone I've ever dated before, so I guess I shouldn't be surprised she hasn't turned around and grabbed my cock yet. It's just that the view usually does a better job than it is now.

"So what do you want to do?" I whisper near her ear.

She smells like some soft, flowery perfume, and I take a deep breath to inhale it into me. Everything about Hailey seems soft. I like that.

"This is nice. We can stay here," she says in a quiet voice.

I brush my lips against her skin just below her ear and feel her breath hitch. She ran away once before. Will she do it again now?

As I wait for her to respond, she turns in my hold to face me. Looking up into my eyes, she says, "So I've just about decided that you're not an ax murderer and probably not married, even though that's not one hundred percent. You have a great car, a great place here, and as far as I can tell, you're nearly perfect. So why do you want me?"

After the shock of her words wears off, I smile. "Nearly perfect? What do I have to fix?"

"Nothing. I just didn't want to say perfect because there's nowhere to go after that. You haven't answered my question, Cade."

Now's my chance. I can tell her I lied last night — more of an exaggeration, really — and then everything can be perfect with her. She won't care. It's not like Hailey is one of those women who gives a damn about what kind of job I have.

Or that I have one at all.

The problem is now she's standing in front of me on my balcony looking so kind and understanding that I know as soon as I tell her, she's going to lose that look she has in her eyes. That way she stares at me that says she thinks I'm pretty fucking special.

I like her thinking of me that way. It feels good for once to have someone be interested in me for me, not for my car or my condo or how much money I have. Hailey doesn't seem to care at all about any of that.

So as much as I know I should say something to clear up the tiny misconception she may have about what I do, I can't bring myself to say the words. Not if it means she won't look at me like she is now.

"I want you because you're you. It doesn't go any deeper than that," I say with a smile that hopefully hides that tiny lie hiding out inside me.

She twists her face into an expression of disbelief. "Because I'm me? I'm not anyone. I'm just some girl who bakes stuff for her parents' restaurant hoping it will bring in more customers."

"That's enough for me. I'm just some guy who saw you looking at me through a kitchen door window and liked that."

Hailey looks around the balcony and then fixes her focus back on me. "You have all of this. You drive that great car. You own a club of your own. I'm not exactly the kind of woman anyone would pair with you. You know that, right?"

I inwardly cringe when she mentions the club. "Exactly what kind of woman am I supposed to be with? Who's doing this pairing up? Because they don't have good taste if they aren't putting me with you."

"Stop joking. I'm serious, Cade."

Cradling her face, I kiss her and hope I can quell the doubts she has about us. I might not be all I claim to be, but I'm not lying when I say I like her.

"I don't care who thinks what about us. I wanted

to get to know you from the minute I met you the other day. You seem to like me, right?"

Her blue eyes open wide, and she hesitates before nodding. "Yes, I do. I just—"

I cut her off before she can think of another question about us and kiss her again. "No just. I like you and you like me. Enough said. That's all that matters."

In the distance, lightning flashes and she quickly spins around. "Was that lightning? I saw it in the reflection in the glass. Maybe we should go in."

"Only if you want to," happy to be anywhere with her.

Hailey looks back at me, her eyes wide. "I forgot. I brought you something. It's in my bag."

As she hurries back inside, I follow behind, curious about what she could have gotten me. "I was wondering why you brought that big bag with you. I thought maybe you were hiding an ax or something."

She smiles at me and shakes her head. "I'm not the ax murderer here."

Reaching into her bag, she pulls out a little white box just big enough to fit a sandwich or a piece of pie. "Here. I saved you the last one."

I open the lid, and there, sitting in the center of the box surrounded by wax paper is a peach colored rose cupcake just as I imagined it would look when she told me all about them last night. "Thank you. I bet it's going to taste incredible."

"It was the last one. When Alex came to see me today, he wanted to try one of the peach cupcakes, but

I had to give him a vanilla rose cupcake instead because this was my last one and I'd put it aside to give you tonight," she says sweetly, but all I hear is Alex went to Comfort Food to see her.

Why the fuck did he do that? Did he go there to try to dissuade Hailey from going out with me because of our argument?

Struggling to control my anger, I say, "Alex came to see you? What about?"

"He wanted to offer me a chance to make desserts for your family's restaurant. I had to turn him down because I don't have the time or facilities, but it was really kind of him to offer."

I push down my emotions and force a smile. "Nothing kind about it. My uncles Cassian and Kane are smart businessmen. They know a good idea when they see one."

For a moment, the two of us stand there silent in my living room as an uncomfortable tension grows between us. It's not Hailey's fault. I know that, but just hearing that Alex went there bothers me after what he said this morning.

"Will you try it? I'd love to know what you think," she says with such hope in her eyes that I can't say no.

I sit down on the chaise part of the sectional I never use and pat the cushion in front of me. "I'm sure it's going to be fantastic. Sit with me."

Opening my legs, I make a space for her. "So this is the last peach rose cupcake? Does that mean they were a hit with your customers?"

I reach in and carefully lift her creation out before

setting the box on the couch to my right. The cupcake almost looks too beautiful to eat, but I can't disappoint her.

"They were," she says, beaming her happiness while I bring the cupcake to my lips. "I hope you like it too."

The first taste of the frosting on my tongue is like pure heaven. Not sickeningly sweet and not stiff like so many cake frostings generally are, it's light and delicious. "This is incredible, Hailey."

"Wait until you taste the cupcake. I put little pieces of real peach in the batter," she says, urging me to continue trying her gift.

I bite into the cupcake, and it's fluffy and just sweet enough. I taste the peach immediately, and smile. "I don't think I've ever had cake that tastes this good. I can see why these sold out today."

Hailey gives me a shy smile and reaches out to drag the pad of her thumb below my bottom lip. "You got icing on your face."

I run my tongue over the spot she touched and want more. More of this cupcake. More of her fingertips drifting over my skin. More of Hailey.

Setting the half of the cupcake left back into the box, I lean forward and press a kiss onto her lips. "Thank you for saving that last one for me."

"You don't want any more of it?" she asks with a hint of hurt tinging her words.

"I'll have more later. Right now, I want more of you," I whisper against her lips.

My cock hardens at the feel of her lips when she

kisses me with all the need and want I give her in my kiss. I want to pull her down on top of me to know what it's like to have the sensation of all of her against me, but I know I have to take it slow or she may run away again. It's like teasing myself, and it's excruciating as each moment passes and all I have is her kiss.

She tentatively touches my chest, her palms pressing gently against my body. It's not enough, but I need to let her set the pace this time. Not my usual style, but I'm willing to do what I have to so Hailey doesn't bolt on me.

Each touch of her fingertips against my shirt drives me crazy. I want her to burrow her hands beneath the fabric so I can feel her skin against mine. When I can't take it anymore, I guide her hands up to my neck and love that first touch of her hands on me.

I lean back, hoping she'll inch her way closer to me, but just then my phone vibrates in my pocket. Fuck. I know who it is without even checking.

"Your phone is making a noise," she says with a smile. "Do you want to take that?"

Shaking my head, I slide my hand around the back of her head and pull her mouth to me. "No. They can wait."

But a few seconds later, my phone vibrates again. Three more times it interrupts us, and I know it won't stop unless I call him back.

"Maybe you should take that. It sounds like someone really needs to talk to you."

I take a deep breath in and let it out slowly as a

combination of anger and frustration fills me. "They don't, but they'll keep calling. Just give me a minute and I'll be right back."

By the time I get into the kitchen, I'm barely able to contain my anger. I know what I'm supposed to be doing tonight. He doesn't have to call fifty fucking times to remind me. It's not that late yet, and that place can do without me for a few more goddamned hours.

Before I can call him back, my father calls yet again and this time I answer it. "You know, calling a dozen times isn't going to make things happen any faster," I say in a low voice. "I'll be there soon."

"You were supposed to be here for eight, Cade. You're an hour and a half late right now, and something tells me you aren't anywhere close to this building."

"I'm coming."

I want to say so much more, but I keep it all in. He wants this from me, but I want something, and right now, that's far more important to me.

"Are you going to be here by ten?" he asks sharply.

"Probably not, but I'll get there. I told you I would."

Lost in my anger at this whole situation, I don't see Hailey standing in the doorway. When I look up at her, she's shaking her head and looks upset.

"I have to go. Bye."

I stuff my phone into my pocket. I hurry to try to explain away the call, but she's already walking away toward the front door.

"I knew you were too perfect to be real," she says with so much sadness in her voice that my chest hurts just hearing it. "I'm going, Cade. Goodbye."

She doesn't get to the door before I catch up with her. "No, don't go. That wasn't anything. I'm sorry they interrupted us. Let's go back and pick up where we were."

Hailey spins around to face me and shakes her head at me again. "Who was that? It sounded like a wife or a girlfriend. I'm so stupid. Why would anyone like you want someone like me? All my joking about red Jag girls. You already have one of those. Just wanted to go slumming for a little while? Was that what I was? And I was so naïve to fall for it all. You must think I'm just some moron, don't you?"

I open my mouth to tell her that call was definitely not from the wife or girlfriend I don't have, but she doesn't give me a chance to get a word in. When she finishes, she turns to leave again, but this time, I grab hold of her arm.

"Let me go! I'm leaving!"

"Don't. I swear. That wasn't a wife or girlfriend. Honest. I don't have either. And none of what you said is right. I like you. Why can't you believe that?"

She rips her arm from my hold and shakes her head, but this time her eyes are full of tears. "Why? Because I know what I look like, Cade. I know what I do for a living. You're not the first guy I've ever wanted to be with who was just playing. I just didn't think I was stupid enough to fall for this trick again."

I stare at her in confusion, knowing I should tell

her just how beautiful she is and how much I like being around her. That isn't what I want to do, though, and why should I? It hasn't worked yet.

Actions speak louder than words, and I'm done talking.

Pulling her to me, I kiss her hard on the mouth and stuff my hand into her hair to keep her where she needs to be. I'm done with this pretending we just like one another and it's enough to just hang out on the couch watching TV.

That's not what I want, and by the way she's reacting to a simple call, that's not what she wants either.

CHAPTER FIFTEEN

ailey

CADE'S KISS TAKES ME BY SURPRISE, AND FOR A FEW seconds, I don't know how to react. I don't believe that call was to a friend or one of his cousins. I have no idea if I'm right about him having a girlfriend or a wife, but the last thing I want to do is kiss him right now.

Except the way his tongue glides over mine, teasing me with a promise of how incredible it would feel on every other part of my body, makes pulling away so hard.

He holds me against him tightly, like if I wanted to leave I couldn't. A mixture of fear and desire overwhelms me, and I don't what to do.

When he lifts his head and smiles down at me, it's almost like he's taunting me. Like he was talking to his girlfriend or wife and now he thinks he can have me too.

Not so quick there, loverboy.

"Thanks for the kiss. I have to go. Bye, Cade," I say and hope my legs weak from that kiss let me walk out the door with some grace.

"No. I'm not letting you run away again, Hailey. You want me, and I want you. Stop trying to fight that."

"I'm not fighting anything that shouldn't be fought. I can't be with you. Goodbye."

Still, he won't let me go.

"You can and you want to be. Why are you acting like this isn't what you want? We had fun talking last night. You brought me that cupcake because you like me. Why fight this?"

"Because you have a girlfriend! Or even worse, a wife!" I scream, hating that everything he says is how I feel and still I know I have to leave.

He reaches into his pocket and pulls out his phone. "Here. Look at who the calls were from. Look at who I called."

Pushing his hand away, I shake my head. "No! I don't want to be that person who doesn't trust someone like that. Just let me go."

But he won't give up.

"Take it. Look. You accuse me of doing something I'm not, so let me show you you're wrong."

God, I don't want to do this. Not here. Not now. Not ever. I swore I'd never let myself be in another situation where I suspected someone was cheating and didn't listen to my gut. Well, at this moment standing in this hallway, my gut says this man is too perfect and now I know why.

When I refuse to take the phone out of his hand, he taps on the screen to bring up the calls. Holding the phone in front of me, he says quietly, "Not a girlfriend or wife. Just my father."

I look at the screen and see one word listed down the screen. Dad. Dad. Dad. Dad. Dad. Dad.

"All those calls were from your father? Is anything wrong?"

Not that I have any right to be asking that, but I suddenly feel so bad for the way I've acted in the past ten minutes that I have to say something.

Cade's shoulders sag, like the weight of my question is a heavy burden on him. "No. That's just the way he is," he says with a sigh.

Knowing the truth makes knowing what to say impossible now, so I mumble the only words I can think of to escape this humiliation I've brought on myself. "I'm sorry. I better go."

"Still? I didn't lie, Hailey. There's no one else, and still you want to run away?" he asks in a voice that fills me with regret.

I hang my head, unable to face him now. "I'm the problem, Cade. That's always how it is. This is all me, and I'm sorry."

As much as I hate to admit the truth, there it is. He isn't the one who caused all of this tonight. It's me. It's always me, and no matter what Dr. Thorpe or

Meadow thinks, I'm obviously still not able to trust like someone like Cade deserves.

This time, he doesn't stop me when I turn toward the door, but behind me, he says, "Don't go. I don't know what happened before you met me, but you can trust me. I won't do whatever they did."

I stare at his front door and want to believe him. I'm so tired of being this way. I want to be happy. I want to have fun. I want to believe all men aren't liars and cheats. Being afraid is so exhausting.

With a heavy sigh, I turn around and see Cade's smile. Not the sexy one that makes me think of all the delicious things I would love to do with him, but the sweet one that lights up his dark brown eyes.

"Why would you want to be bothered with someone who's so fucked up?"

And there is the question I've asked myself every moment since he and I started talking.

Cade steps toward me and stops before taking my face in his hands. Tilting my head back, he looks down into my eyes as I try to push away the urge to run. "Everyone's got something they're fucked up about, Hailey. I'm not afraid of yours, if you aren't afraid of mine."

I close my eyes and let the warmth of his skin against mine course through me. It's gentle but protective, and I want to believe in it.

"Yours? What are you fucked up about?" I whisper.

His lips brush mine, and he kisses me instead of answering. I don't believe he's like me. He doesn't fear everything and everyone, no matter how hard he tries not to like I do.

But at this moment, I don't want to think about that. All I want to think about is how incredible it feels to be kissed like this by someone like Cade.

MY HAND IN HIS, WE WALK BACK THROUGH THE apartment, neither of us saying a word. My insecurities run through me like rampaging villains, tearing up all the sweet thoughts I have about what's about to happen and replacing them with doubts that begin to eat at me even before we reach the bedroom.

I try to stay quiet, to not give voice to the ugly things they whisper in my head, but I can't stop myself, even as I know I may ruin this night for the second time. "I don't know about this, Cade."

He closes the door behind us, and in the dim light coming through the window, I see him smile at me. "I do. It's okay to let someone in. It doesn't always end bad."

As much as I want to believe that, my past says he's wrong. But now as I watch him slowly unbutton his dress shirt and shrug his shoulders to free himself from it, I want to let him in.

How could any sane woman not want that? The body only hinted at through his clothes now stands before me, muscular and tattooed and utterly beautiful.

My gaze drifts over his shoulders and chest while I try to make out the designs of each tattoo on his skin. A bright blue star on his chest. A grey and black design that looks foreign or tribal and covers from his shoulder down to his left ribs. A phoenix or some kind of bird with beautiful feathers of black and red across his stomach.

The urge to reach out and touch those images he's created on his body overcomes me, and I extend my hand to brush my fingertips over the area just between the muscles that create a pronounced V near his hips. Toned, it's divided in half with a thin line of dark hair that continues beneath his pants. His soft skin quivers beneath my touch, a movement that surprises and charms me.

A low moan escapes from his throat, like the sound an animal makes when he's sizing up his prey, and I see in his expression a darkness full of need. "See the effect you have on me?"

I shake my head, utterly unsure of anything but effect he's having on me. Still fully dressed, I stare in awe at how beautiful he is before me.

Cade unzips his pants and they hang open just enough to hint at what lies behind them. I wait for him to take them off, but instead, he crouches down in front of me and runs his hands over my dress.

"You have no idea how beautiful you look sitting there on my bed. I've wanted this since that first day I saw you."

Those doubts in my head grow louder now as my insecurities scream that's all he ever wanted from me. But is that so bad? Is it so bad for a gorgeous man to want me for sex? He could have wanted me for money, not that I have any. Or any other reason that would give me no pleasure.

There are far worse things than a man like Cade wanting to sleep with me. I tell myself that as he slides his hands under my dress and up my thighs. His strong hands press against my skin, exciting me with his mere touch.

"You're not talking. Is that good or bad?" he asks and stops right before he gets to where I so desperately want him to be.

"Neither," I answer with a smile as the last of my doubts return to their usual hiding places inside me.

Cade lifts himself to kiss me softly and whispers against my lips, "You don't have to be afraid, Hailey. I promise I'm not hiding any axes."

"I thought men didn't like when women laugh at times like this, but you're telling jokes."

Leveling his gaze on me, he gives me a wicked grin. "I'm not worried about you laughing. I just wanted to see you smile."

He doesn't give me a chance to say a word before he moves his hands to the inside of my thighs. Every cell in my body comes alive when his thumbs graze the front of my panties, sending a shot of electricity straight to my clit. Cade watches my reaction, smiling at his effect on me, and touches me again, making need surge inside me.

I'm wet, and he knows it. That very fact frightens me because it makes me vulnerable. What if he's just toying with me to see if he can get me excited to want him but he doesn't want me? Is that why he's still wearing his pants?

God, don't let me ruin this, please! No man, no matter how stunning he is, does anything like that. Only in my insecure head does that kind of thing even exist.

Sex is always something men want. A woman wanting it too isn't a problem for them.

All of this races through my mind as he stands up and plants his hands on the bed near my head. Leaning down, he begins to kiss me and lowers his body on top of mine, making sure not to crush me. I feel his hard cock nudge against my hip and react, letting a moan out at what's coming.

"You're so sweet. I bet you taste like heaven on my tongue," Cade whispers in my ear before sliding down my body.

He slips my panties down my legs and licks his lips. I want to say something sexy, something confident that will make him want me more, but my brain is empty. Blank. A void. It's like the mere thought of him going down on me has rendered me mindless.

His hands push my dress up over my waist, and with one last sinful grin, he looks up at me. "Let me hear the wild woman I know lives inside you come out."

A second later, the first flick of his tongue against my pussy makes my eyes roll back in my head. The beautiful mouth that made my legs go weak from his kisses playfully teases me, sucking my clit and running his tongue the length of me so all I want to do is beg him for more.

His left hand presses on my thigh, forcing me open for him, and I arch my back, whimpering with every time he drags his tongue over my clit. Lost in my own delirium, I feel his finger pass over my lips, and a second later when he sinks his teeth ever so slightly into the tender skin between my legs, I suck his fingertip into my mouth. He tastes sweet, like the peach cupcake I saved just for him.

When his other hand leaves my leg, I feel relief for the briefest of moments, but then my need and desire come crashing through me with one finger slid inside me. I suck his forefinger harder, desperate for something to ground me as my body begins to feel like I'm flying with every flick of his tongue and every stab into my wet and willing body.

Moaning against my skin, he adds a second finger and begins to fuck me as he concentrates his mouth on my clit. I arch my back, craving every part of his touch on me to relieve this need, and he pistons his fingers into me faster as he inches me closer and closer to release.

My hips ache my legs are open so wide, but the pain mixes with the pure pleasure of his mouth on me and his fingers fucking me that I don't care how much it hurts. So close, I rock my hips to get to that sweet point, wanting the release of all that's been pent up inside me.

With one last flick of his tongue, I see fireworks behind my eyes and suck hard on his finger as I come with abandon like I've never done before. I cry out in pure ecstasy, and Cade rides each wave of my orgasm, his mouth and tongue lapping against me and creating new aftershocks one after another.

Finally, I wriggle out from under his hold when I can't take it anymore. "I think you're going to kill me if you keep going."

He lifts his head and licks his lips. With one of his wicked smiles, he sighs and says, "Just as sweet as I thought. Like heaven."

"Did you get some kind of specialized training or something in that? I think you might be a master at it," I say and feel my cheeks heat up.

Cade instantly notices and points up at me. "I love that you're turning red right now. I was just between your legs eating your pussy, but asking me that question makes you blush."

I cover my face, embarrassed at my body's need to do that. "Is there anything you can't do?"

He climbs up onto the bed next to me and pries my hands away so I can't avoid seeing him. "I can't make things like you do. I'm afraid I'm going to have to live with just being a sex god."

"Oh, so now you're a sex god? Such an ego, Cade March. Pretty cocky."

With a wink, he says, "It's not cocky if it's true. Then it's just facts. Just wait until next time. You'll see."

Disappointment tears through me. We're not doing anything more?

"Next time? Is this time over?"

He sighs and nods. "Yep. That phone call put a definite end time to this date, but I promise the next one will go as long as you want."

I try to imagine that and smile. "As long as I want?"

With one of those wicked smiles, he nods. "I promise. I'll go as long as you want me to."

When I first met Cade, I had a sense he was one of those men I should be afraid of. I was wrong in one sense, but in another very real way, I should be afraid. Any man this charming and this good with his tongue to make you want more of him that his leaving early disappoints you is a very dangerous man.

And if I'm not careful, I'm going to fall madly in love with him, no matter how much I don't want to.

CHAPTER SIXTEEN

ade

WHEN I WALK INTO CLUB X THREE HOURS LATE, I'M happy with what happened with Hailey tonight and pissed I had to cut short our night together. Sort of a mixed blessing, except I didn't get to come and I'm putting the blame on my father for that.

Blue balls, courtesy of your family. That's some shit I'm going to need a therapist for, no doubt.

The place is packed, as usual, and the crowd in front of the main bar downstairs looks like it's about to crush Cici and Cam. The newest bartenders, from what I gathered from my conversation last month with my father, they don't seem to have matured well behind the bar in the past few weeks. She looks practically dumbstruck trying to serve the next customer, and he appears to have a single speed.

Slow.

Like turtle slow. In a club like this one, that shit doesn't play. Not for long, anyway.

I see the legendary Stefan March come out of his office, look around, and set his eagle-eyed gaze on me, and I know he wants to talk. He always wants to talk. You'd think my interest in getting behind the bar to help his newbies would overrule his need to lecture me about being late, but I can tell by the disgruntled look on his face as he weaves through the crowd that he's in a talking mood.

Or maybe a yelling mood.

"Cade, I want to talk to you," he says when he gets about three feet away from me.

I point toward his hapless workers and say, "Can we do this after I rescue those two? They've got a line three people deep and ten people long wanting drinks. Who's setting up your shifts here these days? Whoever it is, they need to be retrained or fired."

His eyes narrow at my attack on his scheduler, who I know is him. It's always him. He likes being a hands-on kind of owner, and while that's not a bad thing, he's slipping if he thinks these two are up to the job of the main bar.

"Maya is on her break. They'll be fine once she gets back," he says defensively, and I know I've struck a nerve.

"Then I'll take over until she comes back from her break. I'll come to see you in the office then," I call back as I stride away toward the bar.

I know he hates that I just basically dismissed him,

but what he hates even more is the idea that his bar isn't being manned properly. I can fix that, at least. Everything else between us tonight will go to hell pretty quickly once I step into his office, but at least I can get his main source of income here straightened out in the meantime.

As I come around the corner of the bar, I flash a blond in my way a smile and announce, "Ladies and gentlemen, what are we all drinking?"

They all call out drinks and I laugh that no one got the joke. Okay, I guess it was an inside thing. Cici and Cam look at me like they aren't sure if I'm there to help or cause a hassle, so I call them in toward me.

"Cici, take the end of the bar down there. Don't get flustered. Just do one drink at a time, and do it as fast as you can. Cam, you do the middle third, and I'll do this end down here. Don't worry about how many people there are. They all want drinks, so they'll wait a minute. Just don't make them wait two. Okay, let's go!"

They scurry away to where I've told them to go, and I turn to see the pretty blond giving me the eye. "What can I do for you tonight, beautiful?" I ask and get a sexy smile in return.

"Moscow mule. I'm Kirsten. What's your name? Superman come to save the day?" she yells over the crowd cheering about something a few feet away.

I toss her a smile and nod as I begin to pour her drink. "Feel free to call me Superman. Give me a few seconds and I'll have you taken care of."

"Are you the man in charge?" she asks, and I shake my head.

"Not me. I'm just some off-the-street guy come to do a little bartending. The guy in charge is wearing the black suit and green tie and looks like he doesn't know what a good time is," I say, leaning over to place her drink in front of her.

She slides me a twenty and a piece of paper before flashing me another smile. "Well, Superman, keep the change and give me a call sometime. I'd love to see what kind of other superhero feats you can perform."

I could explain to her that I've got someone, even though I'm not sure that's the God's honest truth about what Hailey and I are doing, but what's the point? This is a bar, the blonde wants to flirt, and I'm a bartender whose job is to make customers happy. So I smile and give her wink.

"Time for me to go save more citizens of Metropolis."

With that, I make my way to the cash register and give the mighty Stefan March his take and pocket the ten I made with just a smile and a little sweet talk. It's too bad I hate doing this job. It's not hard and I could probably haul away half a grand tonight, if my father hadn't scheduled Maya too. Why does he insist on having me come in if he doesn't need me?

Well, he needs me, but that would mean sending poor Cici and Cam home. But my father has other plans for me, I'm sure.

Twenty minutes later, my third of the bar has more people than the rest of it because my two co-workers took my pep talk and disregarded every word. I'm halfway to what I might have made all night because of them, so I guess I can't be too disgusted with how bad they are at this job.

I'm not the one who's in charge of who works and who gets fired here, but if I was, they'd both be gone.

"Stefan Junior," a voice says behind me, and I turn to see Maya back from her break.

She knows I hate that little swipe she takes at me every time we meet up. One month of working together and she thinks I'm as bad as my father. I'd get rid of her too if this was my place, but not because she's shitty behind the bar. She isn't. In fact, she's been known to be damn good sometimes and the customers love her.

I'd get rid of her because she insists on calling me that little name.

"Maya, how great to see you again," I coo, obviously not happy to see her. "Taking half-hour breaks now? Seems pretty early in the night. Boyfriend couldn't wait?"

And that's my swipe back at her. I know her boyfriend broke up with her last month. My father had to babysit her weepy ass for a week because she couldn't keep it together. Yours truly got to fill in for her then too and got to have the privilege of seeing how kind the great Stefan March could be to someone who isn't me.

Maya's green eyes open wide at my insult. "Fuck you, Cade! Get out of my way. This is my bar tonight."

Taking a fifty from my final customer, I head toward the register and get him his change. When he kindly leaves me a ten for a tip, I pocket that and look over at her.

"Then act like it so I don't have to come in here and clean up your fucking mess. You used to be good behind the bar. Maybe you could try to be that again."

Before she can clap back with some attempt at a witty retort, I slide around the edge of the bar and head into the crowd. Not two steps toward the stairs, I see my father wave me over toward him as he stands outside his office.

So much for getting away unscathed.

By the time I reach him, my stomach's in a knot and I'm preemptively hating the conversation we're about to have. He gives me a scowl and heads into the office with me following.

"I see you and Maya haven't made up. I thought you two would have been able to get past what happened last summer by now. It's been nearly a year," he says as he walks over to his chair behind his desk.

"Well, she's the same person she was, and I'm the same person I was, and the problem is still there, so I don't know why you would think we'd get past anything by now, Dad."

He leans back in his chair and takes a deep breath in. After he lets it out so slowly that I'm wondering if he's counting back from ten before he explodes, he points at the chair in front of his desk.

"Take a seat, Cade. No need to stand."

I prefer to stand because standing is one step

closer to walking, which is what I want to do at this moment. After a great time with Hailey and a decent time working the bar, the last thing I want tonight is to sit here in this office and listen to another one of my father's lectures.

But I do as he says because it's easier than fighting him. I know how to pick my battles, and whether or not I bother to sit isn't one worth anything.

"You looked good out there. As soon as you got behind the bar, things started working a hundred times better. Those two took your guidance, and the customers love you," he says with a broad smile.

I think this is his way of complimenting me. That's not a bad thing, but I have a sense he might be going for the compliment sandwich thing tonight, so that means what's coming next won't be so wonderful.

"It's not rocket science, Dad. You smile, you flirt, you pour drinks. People pay you, and if you've made them feel good, they give you some money to take home. As for Frick and Frack out there, they might be better at one of the other bars. Maybe the back bar that gets less traffic. Or even better, the second floor bar away from the bathrooms. Maya has no customer skills whatsoever, but people seem to tolerate her. I still don't know why."

He sighs again, this time letting the air out in a rush. "Your mother was always an incredible bartender too, and she never wanted to do that either. I guess you take after her."

Well, this might not be horrible after all. Usually when he brings my mother into the conversation, he's feeling good about something. I definitely want to keep her as the topic, at least for the moment.

"How is Mom? I haven't talked to her in over a week. Is she busy at school?"

My father nods and his expression changes to that one he always wears when he talks about my mother's work. As much as he has no real idea what she's working on when it comes to the specifics of her research, he's proud of her and that shows all over his face.

"She is. I'll tell her to call you when she gets a chance. You know how she is when she's in the middle of her research. I'm sure you'll hear from her soon, though."

The two of us sit there with his desk separating us, two men looking at one another and seeing very similar faces. My father and I look so alike that no one could ever wonder if we're related. Like him, I have dark hair and brown eyes, different from his brothers and their blue eyes. We take after my grandmother and her side of the family, while Cassian and Kane take after my grandfather's side.

All of this wanders through my mind as I sit and wait for him to lower the boom on why he insisted on dragging me in here to talk to me instead of just letting me work like I'm supposed to. I'm assuming I'm going to get the lecture about not being late, but with my father, you never know what he's going to be unhappy about.

"So I hear you have a girlfriend," he finally says, breaking the silence and stunning me at the same time.

Then again, in this family, nothing should surprise me, including Cassian blabbing like some old gossip to my father about what happened at CK the other night. Or was it Alex? He seems to be full of opinions on my life lately. Maybe he shared some of those with my father.

"Really? The March family gossip mill running full steam these days?"

He throws his head back and laughs at my snappy question. "You know how this family is, Cade. I saw your uncle and Alex yesterday and Cassian mentioned to me that you were at the restaurant to see some girl. From what Alex says, she's a gifted chef. Impressive."

Great. So it was both of them. Like father, like son. At least in their case.

"Is that what you called me in to talk about? Because I'm not sure I'd call her my girlfriend. She's someone I'm interested in, and yes, she is talented at her job."

Even as the words leave my mouth, I know I'm acting far too defensive about Hailey. The gossip grapevine in my family is nothing new. Hell, I take part in it from time to time myself. It's not really a shock that my uncle or even Alex would mention my interest in Hailey.

"No, it's not," my father says in a much harsher voice than just a few moments ago. "I just liked hearing that you were seeing someone who is so accomplished."

"Since I usually just see untalented sluts?"

My father frowns and lets out another sigh. "That's

not what I was saying. You always think I'm attacking your choices. All I was saying about this girl is I'm glad you're seeing someone who is so successful. You deserve that."

Before I can stop myself, I say, "She isn't successful. She makes desserts at a little hole-in-the-wall restaurant to help her parents with their business."

I don't know why I tell him that. Not that every word of it isn't technically true, but it makes Hailey sound like so much less than she is.

"Well, Alex raved about her. He says she's a first-class chef."

"Well, if Alex says that, then it must be true."

This meeting has quickly gone to hell, and for possibly the first time in my life, I can't blame my father for that. I don't know why, but hearing him mention what Alex thinks of Hailey makes my blood boil. I don't give a fuck what anyone thinks of her. Let them not think of her at all. That would be even better.

A look of sadness permeates my father's expression now as he stares across the desk at me. "Does it always have to be a pitched battle between us, Cade? I just wanted you to know that I'm happy you're seeing someone so wonderful. What's the problem in that?"

I turn away, hating how disappointed he looks at this moment. "No. Sorry. Thanks. Is this what you wanted to talk about?"

Before I look back at him, I hear the emotion has hardened in his voice. "No. The club is celebrating its five year anniversary after the flood, and I need you here at the front bar Friday night. It's going to be huge, like a packed house huge, so I can't have you being late."

Nodding, I turn to face him. "Got it. Friday night. I'll be here by six for the staff meeting."

The look of surprise I get for that I deserve. Even when I worked here full-time, I rarely bothered with attending my father's staff meetings. He loves those things. My mother told me once that he used to run them when he was just the manager of the bar, and since then, he's held one every night before opening. She thinks it's a ritual for him. I think it's his way to show everyone just who the boss is here.

"Great, great! I'll be happy to see you there."

"One favor, though, Dad. Put Maya somewhere I'm not. If that means you put me upstairs and she gets the main bar, so be it. I'm fine with that. Whatever you think works. I just don't want to have to deal with her all night while putting on my good time bartender face."

"Remind me again why she hates you?" he asks, showing hints of that gossip gene that runs so strong in my family.

I tilt my head back to look at the ceiling as I decide just how much I want to tell my father about why one of his favorite bartenders hates his son. She's probably whitewashed the whole story by now, but tonight I'm feeling the urge to spread some truth about that.

With a wince, I say, "Well, she hates me because we slept together a few times and then I broke it off. I generally don't shit where I eat, but she caught me in a moment of weakness. Actually, a few moments last summer after Emma. Once I told her I just wanted to be co-workers, that was it. Now she calls me Stefan Junior whenever she sees me. I personally think you should get rid of her since she's a bitch on wheels to the customers ninety percent of the time, but you seem to favor her."

"Hmmm…Stefan Junior. That doesn't sound complimentary," he says with a laugh before adding, "To either one of us, in fact."

"No, it doesn't. So that's why Maya hates me and why if you want your big celebration to go smoothly, you'll keep us separated."

With a nod, he says, "Fine. You'll be at the main bar, and I'll put her at the back bar. To keep her happy, I'll make sure something big happens back there so she doesn't think she's being punished."

As much as I shouldn't comment out loud on him keeping her happy, I can't stop myself. "God forbid she think that being a shit to your only son would get her punished."

My father ignores that broadside and smiles. "That's all I wanted to talk to you about. Any chance we'll get to see your girlfriend Friday night? I'll be happy to let Tannick at the door know so she and any guests she wants to bring will get V.I.P. passes."

The very thought of Hailey here at Club X makes the top of my head feel like it's going to blow off. No. Not in this life or the next one. Not even in a third fucking lifetime would I want her to be here while I have to work.

"She's got a lot going on, Dad. She's pretty shy, too. I don't think this would be her thing."

The disappointment returns to his face. "Oh, okay. I'd love to meet her, and I thought here at the club would be a nice casual way that could happen. Your cousins Alex and Cash are planning to come, and I think Kane said Liam would. I'm not sure about Wilder, though."

I stand to leave, already uncomfortable with how much my family is interested in Hailey. "No one is sure about Wilder, Dad. He's still messed up from everything. If that's all, I'm going to go back out there and see how the second floor is faring."

That gets me a huge smile from him, like I've just announced I know the way to bring in a million bucks a night. "What's that face for?"

My father shrugs, still beaming that silly smile. "I didn't even have to tell you where to go. You just knew. No matter if you want to accept it or not, you're a natural, Cade."

I don't bother replying to that. Choosing to check the upper level isn't rocket science. I already know the main bar and the back bar are doing fine. It's only logical to head upstairs.

That's not being a natural at anything here. He just wants to think that because he hopes I'll take after him some day.

Never going to happen.

CHAPTER SEVENTEEN

ailey

MY PHONE BUZZES ACROSS MY TABLE, AND I SEE Cade's name come up in the center of the screen. I shouldn't be so excited to hear from him, but my heart practically skips a beat and I hurry to clean off my hands before reaching for the phone to read his message.

I'm sitting in a booth wishing the world's best cupcake maker was sitting with me.

That's so sweet. Where is he?

I begin to type out my question, but I stop and run to look out the window into the dining room. There in the booth where I first met him Cade sits smiling at me. He waves for me to come out, and without even checking how I look, I hurry out to join him.

"What are you doing here? I wish you told me you

were coming. I would have come out so you didn't have to sit here alone," I say as I slide into the booth on the other side of the table.

"It's okay. I don't mind sitting here for a few minutes. I was going to mention to your father that I was here to see you, but I didn't see him either. Are you busy?"

I shake my head, and at that moment, I realize I'm still wearing my apron covered in chocolate batter from today's dessert creation disaster. I look down in horror to see it's even worse than I thought.

"Oh, God. I must look like a mess. I'm sorry. I didn't think to take this off before I came out here. I'm glad I sat over here because if I had slid in next to you, you'd be covered in chocolate," I say as my cheeks heat up from embarrassment.

Cade reaches across the table and takes hold of my hand. Instantly, I feel like my anxiety calms. "It's okay. You look great. When are you off work?"

"I don't even know what time it is," I say as I look over toward the big round clock on the wall behind the counter. "It's one o'clock already? Wow, time does fly when you're making a mess."

He laughs at my mistake with the saying. "I'm not sure that's how it goes. What were you making that ended up all over you?"

"Well, I started with these cookies I wanted to try. They came out okay, but I wasn't happy with them, so I threw them away. So then I got really ambitious and tried a chocolate torte with a chocolate glaze and ribbons made of chocolate. The torte worked out, but

I wasn't crazy about the glaze and the ribbons ended up as a disaster."

Pointing at my apron, I say, "Thus the chocolate everywhere."

"I bet the cookies and everything were terrific, even if you did end up wearing most of it."

"I wish. I really wanted that cake to turn out great. It would have looked so incredible in the case, and each piece would have been gorgeous," I say, still disappointed I couldn't get those ribbons to work for me.

"So what time are you off?" Cade asks for a second time.

"I can go whenever I want. I'm not really even an actual employee, to be honest," I explain, letting him know the truth for the first time.

"What do you mean? You work here, even if it's for your family. That sounds like an employee."

I force a smile, but it's always hard to explain that what I do for my parents isn't really work. At first when I came home last summer, having me in the kitchen was a way for them to make sure I was okay. Those days were rough, so leaving me alone wasn't anything either of my parents thought was a good idea.

Out of that grew what I do now. They never meant for it to be permanent or anything, really, which is why whenever anyone says I'm some fancy pastry chef or baker I balk at the very mention of those.

I'm just Hailey, someone who tinkers around with chocolate and ends up wearing it more often than not.

Shaking my head, I ease my hand away from Cade's and put it in my lap. I've dreaded knowing I'd have to admit the truth to him at some point. I guess I thought it might never happen or it would happen later than this.

But after last night, I don't want to lie to him. Not about anything, even what I do here at the restaurant or the reason why.

Unable to look up at him, I stare at the silver and gold design on the table and begin. "I never call myself anything fancy. I know Alex likes to say I'm some kind of chef, but that's not true. I have no formal training, and until last year, all I ever did here was wait on tables sometimes for extra money when I was in high school."

That's the easy part. Now comes the hard part of what I have to say.

"Last year, I was in school for psychology. I was a grad student and life was going just as I planned. Then in a matter of weeks, my life turned upside down."

"What happened?" Cade asks, probably thinking I'm going to say something like I failed a class.

If only it was that simple or that minor.

I look up at him and try to smile, but I can't fake it when I have to tell him the truth about what happened. "I fell apart when something in my life changed."

Those aren't the words I know I should say, but using the word breakdown always sounds so damn pathetic. I don't want to tell him I had a mental breakdown.

He doesn't say anything, but I see on his face he's confused. I don't blame him. I'm almost talking in code because I dread having to admit the truth in case it chases him away.

"This time last year, I was engaged to be married. My life was perfect, at least I thought it was. I was well on my way to the career I'd planned for years, and I had a fiancé who I thought wanted to get married like I did. I found out that wasn't true, though, one night when I walked into his apartment and found him in bed with her."

"Damn, Hailey. I'm sorry."

"I don't remember much after that. I drove back to my place somehow—God only knows how because I was a mess—and I crawled into bed. And then I didn't get out of bed for months. By the time my parents stepped in, I'd lost thirty pounds and I'd failed out of school so I didn't have any money to pay rent or my car payments anymore, so the bank repossessed that."

The look on Cade's face is the one I see when I tell people what happened. Not too many people have gotten the full story, but I always see a mixture of horror and sadness looking back at me. Pity sometimes too. I hate seeing that, but I understand why someone would feel that way when they hear what happened.

Thankfully, I don't see pity in Cade now. I don't think I could handle that.

He remains silent, but nods his understanding. I know why he has nothing to say. I get it. I wouldn't know what to say either if someone told me this story.

But I want him to know the whole truth because if we're going to keep seeing one another, he deserves that from me.

"So since I was such a mess and my parents weren't sure what I'd do if left to my own devices, they had me come here every day to keep an eye on me so I didn't do anything to hurt myself. I wasn't suicidal, though. I just didn't care about myself or if I kept going. I didn't see any reason to."

My eyes fill with tears like they do when I think about those days. Now I can't even imagine feeling that way. I don't know that person I was then, and it hurts to remember how little happiness I had in those days.

"Making sweet things gave me reason to go on. I found some kind of joy in that, so my parents encouraged it. I know it probably sounds strange, like how could that help someone come back from falling apart, but it did. Every day I would come in here and go back to my little spot in the kitchen where I could hide out and play with ingredients to make things. At first, they were just for me and then my parents too, but after a while, I agreed to let them put them out for their customers."

I wipe under my eyes so I don't look like some deranged and sad raccoon in front of Cade. I see him smile at me, but it's not his usual grin.

"You don't have to tell me this if you don't want to, Hailey," he says softly.

"Yes, I do. I want to be honest with you. My fiancé wasn't honest with me, and it crushed me. If he had just told me the truth, I would have been heartbroken, but I wouldn't have fallen apart like I did. Even if you walk out of this restaurant when I'm done and decide never to see me again, I think you deserve to know who you spent your time with."

"I'm not going to do that, so you don't have to worry."

"Well, whatever happens, I want you to know who Hailey Canton is. I see a therapist, and she's been terrific. I know why all that happened now and why I reacted like I did, but I also know it's my defense mechanism to push people away. I've done it with you and every person I've met since all that happened last year. I work on that, on not doing it, but I'm not very good yet. You have no idea how much I wanted to run away last night. If you hadn't kept talking to me when I was at your front door, I would have run, Cade."

A slow smile lights up his beautiful face at my mention of last night, and I assume he's going to say something about what we did. When he doesn't, I know I haven't made a mistake telling him all of this today.

"Well, you ran away on me that day in the parking lot here, so I had a feeling you're a runner. I think I knew if I didn't do something to keep you there last night, you'd never agree to see me again."

"I'm sorry about that. I have trust issues, which sounds like some lame excuse for bad behavior, but I do."

He has no idea how many times I've run away from him in my head. That first day. In the parking lot.

At CK. While we walked that night. When I thought he was talking to a woman on the phone last night. When we were in his bedroom.

Every time I had to fight that familiar impulse to run away when something scared me.

But I don't want to be that scared little version of Hailey anymore.

"It's okay. I like a challenge," he says sweetly.

"I'm not trying to pressure you into anything with all of this. I'm guessing you're feeling pretty overwhelmed by this story, and I don't blame you. Whatever you decide to do with this is okay, Cade. I just wanted to tell you because you deserve the truth."

Whether it's what happened to me or something else, I sense what I've just said bothers him. A look of sadness crosses his face for a brief moment before he makes himself smile, I suspect for me more than him.

"I'm glad you told me, but none of that changes the fact that I like you, Hailey. I also think you're downplaying how talented you are at what you do in that kitchen, but being humble is no crime. So all that said, I'm here, so let's get out of here and have fun."

"How do you know I'm off?" I ask with a giggle.

"You just told me this isn't really a job, so I figured I could steal you away from here whenever I wanted."

"I did, didn't I?" I admit sheepishly. "It's actually sort of a job in that I have to tell my father I'm leaving. Give me a couple minutes to find him and get out of this apron and then I'll be able to leave."

Cade sits back and stretches his arms along the back of the booth. "Then I'll wait."

"Okay. Let me find him and clean myself up."

As I hurry off to the kitchen, I look back to see Cade watching me. He really is a great guy, even better than I expected when I took a chance and didn't run away in CK's parking lot.

I'm glad I told him the truth about what happened with me. He told me the truth last night, so he deserved me being honest with him.

Bursting through the kitchen doors, I call out, "Daddy, I'm leaving for the day. Tell Mom I don't know when I'll be home."

My father pokes his head out from behind a freezer door and nods. "Okay, honey. Stay safe. Are you and Meadow going somewhere?"

With a big smile, I answer his question. "I'm going to spend the day doing something fun with Cade."

I like the sound of that.

CHAPTER EIGHTEEN

ade

"So what should we do first?" I ask as Hailey and I walk toward my building. "Swim or go jet skiing?"

Her eyes grow wide. "I've never gone jet skiing. I don't think I can drive one of those things. I might kill someone."

"Then you can sit behind me and I'll be the one at the controls. You'll love it. It's a good time."

"Are you sure it's not dangerous? I've watched people before doing it. They fly around on the water like maniacs."

Waving away her concerns, I laugh as the memory of the last time Alex and I went out and nearly drowned because of some asshole and his girlfriend playing around out there. Fucking newbies.

I can see she's still worried, so I weave my fingers through hers and bring her hand to my mouth to press a kiss onto her thumb. "I promise it'll be fine. I don't drive like a madman in the Jag, so why would you think I drive a jet ski like that?"

"You do sort of drive like a madman in your car, though, Cade. Didn't you notice me hanging on to the door a few times the other night?"

"No, but I was too busy looking at the woman sitting next to me to notice that. It wasn't that bad. Well, that one turn I took a little fast, but you didn't scream, so I figured I was fine."

She laughs at my explanation, making her look even more beautiful than usual. "That's a weird litmus test you have there for if you're driving too fast."

"I guess I could use someone jumping out of the car, but that wouldn't be fair. No one has ever jumped out while I'm driving. So screaming sounds about right."

"Because someone has screamed before?"

With a shrug, I have to admit the truth. "A couple times. People can be excitable sometimes. I chalk it up to that."

As the elevator doors open, I tug Hailey in and press the button for the fifteenth floor. Alone with her, finally, I slide my arms around her waist and pull her to me. After what she told me back at the restaurant, I feel like I need to make sure she knows I'm not like that asshole who fucked her life up last year.

"We could just forget about doing anything but

hanging out in the house. It's not like we can't go out later. You know, it is pretty hot out today."

She looks up at me and raises her eyebrows. "Have you lived in Tampa a while? It's May. This isn't as hot as it gets."

"I've lived here all my life, actually. I was just looking for an excuse to keep us inside, preferably in bed."

And at that moment, I see suspicion fill her eyes. She thinks I'm a guy who just wants to fuck her and that's it. Smooth, Cade. Real smooth.

I don't give her the chance to pull away or say anything. "I didn't mean that the way it came out. I'm all about jet skiing all afternoon, if that's what you want to do."

"So you don't want to sleep with me? Is that what you mean?" she asks with such innocence that I realize I've gotten myself into a hole I need to get out of quickly.

Shaking my head, I work to change what she's thinking before she bolts as soon as the elevator doors open. "No, no. That came out wrong too. Let me start again. I'd love to spend all afternoon in bed with you, but that's not all I want to do with you. Yeah, that sounds closer to what I meant."

For a few moments, I watch to see if that made things any better, and finally right before the elevator stops on my floor, Hailey gives me one of her sweet smiles. "I knew what you meant. I was just playing with you. You're cute when you're like that, though."

"Like what?" I ask just as the doors open.

"Sweet. Thoughtful. You don't look like you'd be that kind of guy, but you are, and I like that."

The doors begin to close as I lower my head to kiss her, but one of my neighbors stops them and marches into the elevator, interrupting us. It's that guy from across the hall who likes to wear Hawaiian shirts all the time and pulls his hair back into a man bun.

"Oh, sorry. Didn't realize it was that late in the day."

Hailey's cheeks turn bright red, and she hurries out of the elevator while I give him a nasty look on my way out. "Yeah, like there's a time when a guy can kiss someone in here. Aloha, dude."

By the time I get down the hall, she's giggling uncontrollably. "Did you just say aloha, dude to a guy wearing a Hawaiian shirt? What did he say back?"

"Nothing. He's an asshole. Like this is some puritan building that doesn't allow me to kiss you in the elevator. That guy needs to get laid and change his clothes. The seventies want their look back."

As I open my door, she whispers next to me, "Don't be mad. I don't think he meant any harm."

I turn my head so our mouths are just inches away from one another. "He ruined a sexy moment on me. He'll pay in the future. I'll make sure of that. It will be painful and torturous. Maybe it will involve a wreath."

"If I kiss you now, will that spare that man all that pain?" she asks with a gentle smile.

"No, but that's because he's been a Hawaiian shirt wearing dick for years," I say before leaning toward her and kissing her on the lips.

"Hell hath no fury like a man denied a kiss in an elevator," she says as she walks into my place.

"Othello, right? Or maybe Hamlet? Sounds pretty tragic, so I'm guessing one of those," I joke before following her into the living room.

Wrapping my arms around her, I snuggle up to her back and press a kiss to her neck. "So did we decide if we're staying in or going out? I don't remember."

Hailey slides her hands out from beneath mine at her waist and pretends to weigh the choices. "Hmmm...go out and possibly get killed by a maniac driver on a jet ski or stay in and have sex. What's a girl to choose?"

"Just one question before we decide. Am I the maniac driver?" I ask before nuzzling her neck.

Giggling, she wriggles out of my hold and turns around to face me. "Yes, I'm sorry to say you are, so that only leaves us with sex. I hope you aren't too disappointed."

I reach out and pull her back to me, loving how her body feels on mine. "I'll get over it. I can go jet skiing with one of my cousins or my friends."

We stand there with me holding her to me for a while, neither one of us saying a word, and I can't remember the last time I was this quiet with anyone, but especially with a woman. I use talking to get what I want. Always have. It's just how I am.

But with Hailey, I want to be quiet sometimes. Like now, when we're standing in my living room and her eyes are closed and I have a feeling she wants to run.

I have to make it that she can't, though, and I have a feeling that isn't with anything I can say right now.

Finally, she whispers into the silence we've created together, "So you got quiet there. Everything okay?"

"I was just thinking the same exact thing."

She looks up at me and nods. "Yeah, everything's okay."

"Good. I liked that, though."

With a smile that lights up her beautiful blue eyes, she says, "I liked it too. It made me feel calm."

"I thought maybe you might want to run there for a few seconds."

Before she says another word, I know by the look in her eyes she did feel like running. But she didn't, and that's all that matters.

"I did, but I remembered what my therapist told me to do and made a list in my head of all the reasons I shouldn't. Want to know what was on the top of that list?"

For a moment, a flash of doubt crosses my mind and I wonder if I actually do want to know the most important reason why she stayed. That passes, though, and I say, "Yeah."

Taking my hand, she begins to walk us toward my bedroom as I wait for her to give me that reason. When we reach the doorway, she turns around and says, "The number one reason I had for not leaving is after last time, I'd be crazy not to sleep with you. Any man who can do what you did with your mouth has to be good in bed."

I nod, smiling at how cute she is. "Well, I'm glad

you liked my skills. I think you're going to like what I can do with the rest of me too."

"I'm sure I will."

"So what was reason number two?" I ask while I begin to strip her out of her pink T-shirt and jeans shorts.

Looking up, I see her smiling at me when I tug her shorts down her legs. "I'll tell you later."

I don't know why whatever this is between us feels so easy, like it's right that she's here and we're about to sleep together. When I've been with other women, it's never felt wrong but it didn't feel like this.

Sweet. That's what this feels. Sweet, like two people who make each other smile looking to find happiness in one another.

I can't remember any time with a woman before that felt so comfortable like this.

As she steps out of her shorts and kicks them off to the side, I move to her T-shirt, pulling it over her head. She's left standing in matching pink bra and panties, there in front of me with innocence in her blue eyes.

"Not that I wouldn't do this, but I didn't wear these thinking you and I were going to sleep together today. I wish I was that kind of woman, but I'm not that coordinated in the morning."

Glancing up and down her body, I nod my approval. "Whatever reason you did it, I like it. Then again, I'd like you in seaweed underwear and a coconut bra, so keep that in mind."

Hailey scrunches up her face like she just sucked on a lemon. "Seaweed underwear? That sounds gross.

I think you might have just ripped me out of the mood."

I wrap my arms around her and pull her against me. "Then it's my job to get you back in the mood because there's no way we're wasting a fine coordinated underwear and bra day."

She looks up at me like she's studying my face for a long moment. "Are you always this cute?"

"Pro tip: men like to think they're masculine and tough. Being called cute makes us worry we're like puppies, and no guy wants to be like a puppy."

While her fingers fumble with my zipper, she says, "Well, I'm sticking with cute. Funny, cute, and sexy. Any of those work for you, He-Man?"

"I hear women love funny guys. You make a girl laugh and boom! Her panties fall off. So I'll take funny and definitely sexy."

When she reaches inside my pants and palms my cock, I see a sly smile form on her lips. "Still thinking I'm just cute?"

Her tongue glides along her bottom lip and she reaches inside my underwear. The first touch of her hand on my skin makes me hard as a rock, and at this moment, I wouldn't care if she liked me because I have straight teeth.

"Maybe not just cute. You do have some fine attributes. I've got one in my hand right now."

She strokes it from base to tip, making my eyes roll back in my head. "I don't think anyone's every called my cock one of my fine attributes," I croak out, barely able to form the words this feels so fucking good.

I watch in amazement as she lowers herself to the floor and kneels in front of me. "I figure since you did me last time, I should return the favor. You know, since your attribute is so fine and all."

A second later, she wraps her pretty little mouth around my cock and her tongue hits the underside of the head to send me straight to heaven. Instinctively, I stuff my hands into her hair and tighten around the soft blond strands, but then I remember this is Hailey and not one of the usual women I've been known to sleep with.

When I release my hold, she looks up with confusion in her eyes. Leaning back, she eases my cock out of her mouth and asks, "Did I do something wrong?"

"No, not at all. Definitely not. I just didn't want to…"

"You don't have to treat me with kid gloves, Cade. I'm okay."

"Trust me. You're better than okay."

Hailey smiles, and then she returns to sucking my cock. I watch, amazed at how she can be both so sweet and so good at giving head both at the same time. The combination excites me more than I ever imagined possible.

As much as I love the way her mouth feels on me, I want more for our first time together. Next time, she can finish me this way.

Tilting her head back gently, I smile down at her. "Time to switch positions."

Again, she looks confused as I help her up. "Something's definitely wrong, right?"

"No, definitely right, but I have something else in mind," I say while I strip out of my clothes.

"Something else?"

A couple seconds later, I get those pretty pink panties and bra off and kiss her deep, tasting that tongue that made me feel like I'd died and gone to heaven. "Something else, as in you against this wall and me fucking you."

Those innocent blue eyes seem to get a wicked twinkle in them now, and when I lift her up, she wraps her legs around my waist. She's sexy and beautiful, and when she looks at me as I ease her down onto my cock, I'm not sure I can handle how sweet she is.

More times than I want to remember, fucking a woman was nothing but a physical act. A way for me to get off. A good time had by all, but that was it.

With Hailey, this feels different. More, like something was missing all those other times and now I just realize it.

I want something more than just getting off. I want what Hailey makes me feel right now.

Her lips brush the shell of my ear, and she moans softly when I ease out of her and fill her again. "Mmmm...that feels so good. I knew I wasn't wrong about you being just as good at this as you were with your mouth."

Kissing her neck, I say against her skin, "Hold on because you ain't seen nothing yet."

She rakes her fingernails across my shoulders, turning me on even more, and my body kicks into high gear. I thrust into her and she meets my need with her own, rolling her hips and taking all of me. Her body feels fucking incredible, like her cunt was made to fit my cock like a glove. We rock back and forth, in and out with a perfect rhythm like we're in sync from the start.

Our bodies are damp with sweat, but I could fuck her all day. She kisses me hard on the lips and moans into my mouth, and a second later, that snug cunt of hers tightens even more around my cock and she comes with a squeal of satisfaction that sounds like music to my ears.

A few thrusts later, I come and then sag against the wall, holding her to me as we both fight to catch our breath. Our fucking was all I had hoped for and even more because of Hailey.

Gently, she runs her fingertips over the back of my neck, teasing the drenched ends of my hair. "That was incredible. I don't think my legs work, though, so you might have to carry me over to the bed."

I lean back and smile at her compliment before pressing a soft kiss onto her forehead. "That was incredible. Next round will be on the bed then so your legs can recover."

Her cheeks pinken from a blush at my mention of us going again, and when I lay her down onto the bed, she pulls me down on top of her. "Time for round two?"

"Definitely."

I ease into her again and roll over onto my back so

she's on top of me this time. She looks like a fucking goddess sitting on me with my cock inside her. Setting my hands on her hips, I keep her still for a moment so I can take in how beautiful she is.

Pulling her mouth down to mine, I kiss her and whisper against her lips, "Promise me you won't run."

Her hair drapes over me, tickling my skin, and she pushes it off her face so I see the fear in her eyes. "I'll try not to. I can promise that."

"I'll take it."

It's a start to something I can't believe I even want, but with Hailey, everything seems different. Good. I've had enough of the way my life was going.

CHAPTER NINETEEN

Cade

MY FATHER BEAMS A SMILE THAT COULD LIGHT UP A small city as he explains to the crew for the night that this fifth anniversary celebration is going to be the biggest ever. Some local media is due to arrive at any minute, and people are already lined up on the sidewalk outside dying to get in here and drink until they black out.

"So I want to see you have a good time tonight because without you, Club X wouldn't be here. Smile, enjoy yourself, and make those customers see why you're the best in the business, okay?"

Everyone around me yells and claps, and I join in when I see him looking at me like I'm ruining his big night by not being as enthusiastic as the rest of these people. Why not, right? I'm happy and loving life, so why not give my father some bit of happiness too?

"Any problems, you know to see your section leaders or me, but see them first," he says, and everyone laughs.

"Okay, have a great night!"

More clapping before the crowd of my co-workers breaks up and people start their prep to get ready for opening. Even though I made it for his nightly pep talk, I don't know where he's got me scheduled, so I follow him into his office.

"Cade, what can I do for you?" he asks as he rifles through a stack of papers.

"Not sure what you want me to do tonight."

He looks up and smiles like he's thrilled about what he has to tell me. "Oh, I want you up at the main bar, for sure. I want you playing to those people here from Tampa Scene Magazine. Lots of smiling and do that thing you used to do with the bottles. People love that."

"I didn't realize people still read magazines."

My father rolls his eyes. "It's online. They just call it that, I guess. I don't really know, to be honest. I just know that the publicist I hired for this has all these people coming in to take pictures and record videos of the crowd to put all over social media. She also has them doing other things I don't really know about, so if someone sticks a phone or a mic in your face tonight, turn it on like only you can, okay?"

Thank God I had six cups of coffee today or I

wouldn't be of any use to him for this anniversary shindig.

"Got it. Turn on the charm. Anything else?"

He thinks for a second and shakes his head before something comes to him. "Oh, yeah. Is that girlfriend of yours coming tonight?"

Something in the way he calls Hailey my girlfriend makes me bristle at the very sound of it, and I shake my head. "She's not coming, no."

"Fine. Then you'll be able to be the guy you were last summer?"

I nod, not really sure what he means by that. "Yeah, I guess. I might be a little taller. I think I had a growth spurt this year."

"Stop busting my chops, Cade. I've got about three million things going on right now. You know what I'm talking about."

Yeah, I know. I didn't want to think about it, but I know.

"Sure. I'll be that guy for you tonight."

"Great. Now have a good time and come find me if you run into any problems. I put Maya at the back bar and made sure we've got a bunch of promo shit going on back there, so she'll be happy. Cici and Cam are at the upstairs bar that gets the least amount of business. And you're at the main bar with the twins."

"Katelyn and Kalli?" I wonder aloud, not sure those are even their names. It's been a few months, and everyone just calls them the twins.

My father thinks for a minute, as if he isn't sure of their actual names either. "Kalli? I think it's Kylie."

"So Cade, Katelyn, and Kylie at the main bar. Going for a theme?"

He shakes his head, clearly not amused by my question. "I'm going for the two most gorgeous females behind the bar and the one and only Cade March. Your reputation precedes you. Use it to your advantage."

"My reputation precedes me? I haven't tended bar on a regular basis here for nearly a year, Dad. I doubt anyone even remembers me. You're going to have a hell of a lot more success with the twins, I think."

"Don't kid yourself. I've been in this business a long time. I know when someone is memorable."

Now it's my time to not be amused. "I think you might be biased then. Put your faith in the twins."

As I make my way toward the door, he says, "One of the people from that magazine or whatever it's called remembered you, so I think you made an impression on her, at least."

"I think she has me confused with someone else. No matter. Everyone will get the guy they're expecting, and the twins and I will have the main bar rocking."

"Good! See? You're a natural at this."

He wishes I was. I wish I was back at my place with Hailey. Neither one of us gets what we want tonight.

MY FATHER DIDN'T EXAGGERATE WHEN HE SAID IT would be a celebration. By ten o'clock, people stand shoulder to shoulder in front of the bar, and the twins and I barely have time to catch a breath between customers. I see a hand go up at the end of the bar and hurry down to find the March and Jackson family contingent fresh in the door and thirsty.

Alex drops a hundred on the bar in front of me and smiles. "Are we still being a bitch about things, or should we find one of the other bars?"

I take his money and hand it back to him, shaking my head. "Fuck you, and your money's no good here tonight. If the almighty Stefan March insists I work this hoedown, then my family and friends drink for free."

His brother Cash leans in and looks at me with that intense blue-eyed stare so like his father's. "Planning on bankrupting your father before he forces you to take over the place?" he asks and then laughs. "If I had known tonight was free, I would have better prepared. How've you been, Cade? Alex tells me your father is pulling hard on the reins lately."

I shake my head at him and roll my eyes. "Everyone in this family is like fucking hens. All you do is gossip." Turning to look at my cousin Liam, I say, "Let me guess. You know all my goddamned business too, right?"

My uncle Kane's older son, he's quiet like his father, something I appreciate since it usually means he's not interested in the family bullshit. But tonight, it seems even Liam is here to bust my balls.

With a shit-eating grin, he answers, "You know how fast word travels in this family. Don't worry, though. Looks like you got yourself a job, so your father will get off your back. Speaking of that, do you serve drinks at this job, or do you just talk to people dying of thirst?"

All three of them laugh, but I get it. As close as we've all been all our lives, it's not surprising they think they should ride me about my father's latest scheme to get me to run this place. I should have expected them to show up and act like they are.

"Fuck you guys, and if you aren't careful, I'll let the twins handle you."

My cousins turn their heads and look down the bar at the two gorgeous bartenders I get to work with tonight. Both have their blond hair up in ponytails, and both are wearing shirts that I'm pretty sure defy the laws of nature, or at least fabric, and show off as much of their tits without being naked.

"Christ, what is the tensile strength of those buttons?" Cash asks as the three of them stare at exactly what both twins hope male customers will notice and pay nicely to see as they get their drinks tonight. "They have to be super glued because there's no way that one little button is holding back all of that."

Liam smiles, and Alex taps me on the arm to get my attention. "I think you misunderstand the idea of punishment, man. There's no reason for us not to bust your ass all night long if we get them instead of you."

"Fuck off. Now you get whatever I decide to pour you three."

I leave them staring at the twins' assets and return

a minute later with three whiskeys. When Alex doesn't see one for me, he stops his brother and Liam from taking a drink.

"First drink, you have to join us. It's a tradition."

"I can't get hammered tonight. There are like a million fucking people here. This job gets hard when your head is up your ass."

"One drink," Cash says, egging me on like he usually does. "You won't even feel it."

Grabbing the bottle off the shelf, I give in and pour myself a glass of whiskey. "One, but then I have to get back to work. What are we toasting to?" I ask as I lift my glass.

The four of us clink our glasses together, and Alex says with a grin, "To new beginnings."

"To new beginnings," the three of us repeat and then each of us takes a drink.

I know that's Alex's way of saying he's sorry for giving me a hard time about Hailey. I can forgive him. I have to. He's my best friend, and even if I didn't want to let things go, this family isn't going to let that continue on for long.

"We're going to go see what's happening, but we'll check back. Don't work too hard," he says with a laugh.

Since it's better to ignore him as he's just being a bust ass, I head off to get drinks for paying customers. I'll catch up with them later, assuming my father doesn't have me giving interviews to some lame online magazine about how great working at Club X is.

That is definitely not what he wants to happen. I hope he knows that.

AN HOUR LATER, ONE OF THE TWINS LOOKS LIKE SHE needs a break from all the adoration the male customers are giving her. Her smile seems forced, so I head down to her end of the bar to check that she's okay.

Over the music, which has gotten so loud in the past few minutes that I can barely hear myself think, I say into her ear, "Everything okay? You need a couple minutes away?"

I don't use her name because I'm not sure if it's Katelyn or Kylie, but whichever one she is nods and leans in toward me. "Thanks! I just need a minute or two to get some fresh air and maybe splash some water on my face. I won't be long."

"We'll be fine."

"Okay. Thanks, Cade. Kylie still looks like she's going strong, so she'll be good if you get a huge rush, but I promise I won't be long. I'll be back in a minute."

Good to know this is Katelyn. Okay. I quickly scan her face and see she's wearing gold hoop earrings. Turning to look at her sister, I see no hoops. Good. Katelyn is hoops and Kylie isn't. That works.

Not thirty seconds after she walks out from behind the bar, all hell breaks loose. That media person my father said remembered me pushes her way to the front of the bar, and I instantly have a flashback as to why she knows me.

Easter weekend two years ago. Too much tequila. Way too much. A brunette and a redhead, sisters home from college. Or maybe they were on vacation. I didn't pay attention to their story much at the time. I actually wondered if somewhere nearby there was a blonde to round out the look we had going on.

Now the redhead stands in front of me, all smiles with some guy with a camera behind her. How did that weekend turn out? I can't remember, but I don't think anyone left with hurt feelings. Why would they? We were just three people having a good time.

"Cade March, baby, you are a sight for sore eyes. When your father told my producer that his son was going to be the star of this party tonight, I thought he meant you. Seeing you now brings all those memories back of that weekend my sister and I spent with you at the beach. Remember?"

I flash the smile I know I have to and nod like I'm happy to see her. Except I don't know her name.

"How've you been?" I ask, leaving my question hanging in mid-air in the hopes that she'll fill in her name.

She smiles, like she has my ploy all figured out, and leans over the bar to grab my shirt by the collar. Pulling me toward her, she plants a kiss full on my lips.

"Taryn. And I'm great, honey. I'm working with Tampa Scene and we're here to cover this anniversary party that's kicking. I was going to have my guy focus on those gorgeous girls that have been flanking you all night, but now I'm thinking all three of you are better. Sort of like bringing back old memories, right?"

"Great!" I yell over the music and look for anyone needing a drink. "Just let me know what you need."

A minute later, Katelyn returns and I hear over the sound system someone announce that something's happening at the main bar. What the fuck is going on?

I look at the twins, but they shake their heads like they don't have a clue either. I see Alex coming toward me like he needs to talk to me, but before he can reach me, Taryn and her camera guy are making their way around to behind the bar.

"Okay, let's get a shot of you three gorgeous people in your native environment," Taryn says as she directs her guy to stand a few feet back from her.

Kylie eagerly runs over to her and asks, "What is this for? Is this for something in the press?"

As Taryn explains who she is and where she works, Katelyn tugs on my shirt to get my attention. "Cade, what's going on? Your father didn't say anything about people interviewing us."

"It's fine. Just smile a lot and do your job. That's all I plan on doing. Your sister seems happy about this, though."

I see Katelyn shake her head and wonder why she looks so worried. It doesn't take long to find out.

CHAPTER TWENTY

$\mathcal{H}$ailey

I CLING TO MEADOW'S ARM AS SHE MAKES A PATH for us through the standing-room only crowd. Everyone seems drunk and it's so incredibly loud that she can't hear a thing I try to say to her. No wonder I don't hang out in clubs much.

She turns her head and yells, "That announcement said something was happening at the front bar, so let's go there."

Nodding, I tighten my hold on her wrist and hope to God we don't get separated. I have no idea where I'd end up if this sea of people took me away.

We have to stop about ten feet away from our destination when the crowd gets so densely packed that we can't move. Looking back at me, she yells,

"Hold on. I think I see a hole over there near the wall. We might not see everything, but it will be closer."

Unsure if it's possible to be closer to any of these people as their arms and legs rub up against my body while we make our way toward the wall, I weave through those body parts as they flail this way and that with excitement. Finally, I see that hole Meadow mentioned and breathe a tiny sigh of relief. If I can just get a few inches between me and the next person, I'd be happy.

"Tonight, as we celebrate the fifth anniversary of Club X coming back from being underwater, let me hear everyone give a cheer for the hottest club in town!" a female's voice says over the sound system.

Meadow and I stop against the wall as the crowd erupts into cheers and yelling. Hundreds of drunk partiers all at once begin to chant, "Club X! Club X!" It's like nothing I've ever experienced, and after a few times, I start yelling it too.

"Look at you!" Meadow says in my ear.

I turn to look at her and smile. "I'm definitely a fish out of water here, but I figure I should try to blend in. When in Rome…"

"I'm just so glad you agreed to come. When Alex offered me the V.I.P. passes, I didn't know if you'd say yes. It's so great you did! And I love you in that dress!"

She hadn't mentioned if Cade would be here, but I secretly harbored the hope he would since Alex had called Meadow to give her the passes. She didn't know how he'd gotten them, but Meadow is always up for a good time, unlike me.

Tonight is different, though. I feel different. Spending time with Cade has made me feel like a new person, a more confident person.

Not confident enough to ask Meadow if she knew if Cade would be here, though. He told me he had work when I asked him what he was doing tonight, so I probably won't get to see him. But maybe because he's the manager of his own club, he had someone take over since his cousin has tickets to this place.

Of course, all of that stayed in my mind when I was talking to him and Meadow. It's enough that I dressed in one of her tiniest dresses and her heels that are two inches higher than any shoes I've ever worn. I'm not brave enough to let people know how much I love seeing him.

"I don't see Alex anywhere," she says in my ear.

Her disappointment comes through loud and clear. From the moment she laid eyes on him that night at CK, she's been talking about how much she hopes they'll get together. I hope so too since he's a great guy and she's my best friend.

"How can you tell in this crowd? I'd be lucky to find my own hand while we were walking through all those people."

"I know this isn't your type of place, but isn't it great?" she asks just as the woman on the sound system starts talking again. "It's so alive!"

A little too alive for me, but I'm here, so I don't want to ruin her time. Smiling, I point up toward the ceiling and say, "I think they're about to announce something."

"Ladies and gentlemen, tonight at the main bar here we have the most delicious trio you'll ever see. If you haven't met them already, here are the twins Katelyn and Kylie, and sandwiched between them like you know he loves being is the famous, well actually, infamous Cade! Give them a hand and let them know how much you love all three of them!"

The crowd erupts into cheers again, and I crane my neck to see the three beautiful bartenders just described. The twins are stunning with bodies to die for, but I can't see the other one. Just hearing that name makes me wish my Cade was here with me right now.

My Cade. I like how that sounds. But if we could be together right now instead of me being here and him being at work, I'd rather if we were at his place enjoying each other and the silence I never realized I loved until about twenty minutes ago.

Meadow grabs my hand and tugs me away from the wall. "Honey, we have to go. This place is getting too crowded. I feel like we're going to get crushed at any moment. Let's leave and call it a night, okay?"

I love that idea, so I hurry to keep up with her, happy I'll get some fresh air and elbow room once we leave this bar. All around me, people cheer and the sound system begins to play the striptease song. Curious, I look back, wondering if those women actual take their clothes off when they bartend, and what I see stops me cold.

Meadow tries to keep me walking toward the door, but I yank her back next to me as I watch one of the twins and Cade standing on the bar. My Cade. His shirt is wide open, and the woman lowers herself down until she's eyelevel with his zipper. As the crowd cheers her on, she stuffs her hands into his black pants and moves her face toward him. I can't see what she's doing, but everyone around us screams in excitement.

"Honey, why couldn't you just leave when I wanted to?" Meadow asks sadly as tears fill my eyes.

I shake my head in disbelief. Cade doesn't look unhappy that this gorgeous woman with enormous breasts is licking his stomach or whatever she's doing. I can't tell, but I can imagine what a woman does when her face is that close to his crotch.

He lied to me. He said he had to work at the club he manages. He never said he was a bartender and put on whatever the hell kind of show this is for a living. I asked him specifically what he was doing tonight since I didn't want to say yes to Meadow to come to this place if he and I could be together.

Now I know what he had to do that was better than spending time with me.

The woman stands up to her full height and takes a bow on the bar while everyone around us cheers. All I want to do is leave. That and throw up as the memory of finding Malcolm with that woman in the bed we shared fills my head.

All Cade had to do was tell me the truth. Now I can't help but wonder why he lied. Is he with this woman? It sure looks like they know each other well.

Was he talking to her the other night? Was the name Dad in his phone just some decoy to hide that he's with her?

The infamous Cade. Sounds like I'm the only person in this bar who doesn't know who Cade March really is.

God, I'm so stupid. All along, I wondered why he would ever want to bother with me. I pushed that doubt and fear away because Dr. Thorpe and Meadow keep telling me it's not real.

But it is fucking real. It's real and it's standing on the bar in front of me, right now.

Meadow tugs my arm to leave, but right before I start toward the door, I make eye contact with Cade. I instantly see the guilt in his expression. He lied, and he knows he's been caught.

All he had to do was not lie. Why did he lie? Did he lie about everything?

"Come on, Hailey!" she yells, and this time I don't try to fight her.

I don't want to be here anymore. The person I thought was a fun guy who genuinely liked me isn't who he pretended to be.

He lied, and I don't know why.

I just know this hurts.

CADE AND HAILEY'S STORY CONCLUDES IN
INFAMOUS (NeXt #2)
GET YOUR COPY TODAY!

ABOUT THE AUTHOR

K.M. Scott writes contemporary romance stories of sexy, intense, and unforgettable love. A New York Times and USA Today bestselling author, she's been in love with romance since reading her first romance novel in junior high (she was a very curious girl!). Under her Gabrielle Bisset name, she write paranormal and historical romance. She lives in Pennsylvania with a herd of animals and when she's not writing can be found reading or feeding her TV addiction.

Be sure to visit K.M.'s Facebook page at **https://www.facebook.com/kmscottauthor** for all the latest on her books, along with giveaways and other goodies! And to hear all the news on K.M. Scott books first, sign up for her newsletter today and be sure to visit her website at **http://www.kmscottbooks.com**

BOOKS BY K.M. SCOTT:

Crash Into Me (Heart of Stone #1)

Fall Into Me (Heart of Stone #2)

Give In To Me (Heart of Stone #3)

Heart of Stone Volume One

Ever After (Heart of Stone #4)

A Heart of Stone Christmas (Heart of Stone #5)

Return To Me (Heart of Stone #6)

Forever With Me (Heart of Stone #7)

Heart of Stone Volume Two

Hard As Stone (Heart of Stone #8)

Set In Stone (Heart of Stone #9)

Silent As A Stone (Heart of Stone #10)

Heart of Stone Volume Three

All of Me (Heart of Stone #11)

Temptation (Club X #1)

Surrender (Club X #2)

Possession (Club X #3)

Satisfaction (Club X #4)

Acceptance (Club X #5)

Notorious (NeXt #1)

K.M.'S BOOKS ARE IN AUDIOBOOK TOO!